Rita Red

Money, Men and Memories

Rachel J. Verstegen

PublishAmerica
Baltimore

© 2011 by Rachel J. Verstegen
All rights reserved. No part of this book may be reproduced, stored in a retrieval system or transmitted in any form or by any means without the prior written permission of the publishers, except by a reviewer who may quote brief passages in a review to be printed in a newspaper, magazine or journal.

First printing

All characters in this book are fictitious, and any resemblance to real persons, living or dead, is coincidental.

PublishAmerica has allowed this work to remain exactly as the author intended, verbatim, without editorial input.

Hardcover 978-1-4560-4889-1
Softcover 978-1-4560-4888-4
PUBLISHED BY PUBLISHAMERICA, LLLP
www.publishamerica.com
Baltimore

Printed in the United States of America

ACKNOWLEDGMENTS

Scott, Griffin, Alyse, and Mitch, you are my rocks. I thank God every day for each of you. You had my back from the moment I dreamed this crazy dream of writing a book. You graciously allowed me the time to pursue something for myself that I can share with the world. I watch you grow stronger as individuals each day and always want you to remember, I love you, and support you no matter how wild your ride!

Deb, Val, Mary and Patty, I simply adore each of you. Our girls' weekends in Las Vegas come second to none. I thank you for the laughter, hugs, tears, and just plain, crazy times. I owe this book to you, our times together in the past, and the stories yet to come.

David, without your kindness and hospitality there would be no Annual Girls Vegas vacation, and therefore, no stories to share. You have a kind and generous heart. May life bring you the best.

Rita, I miss you every day. You are my role model, my inspiration, and the driving force behind this book. I knew we would see your name in lights one day! Love you Rita B.

To my family and friends who believed in me even when I did not believe in myself; thank you.

Special recognition goes to Joan, my editor and Brad, my line editor for your dedication to making this book the best it could be. Thank you to Chris, for your artistic ideas on the cover. God Bless.

CHAPTER 1

Ily had just finished pulling the zipper around the last corner of her suitcase when a horn blast from the driveway called out to her. The sound rang from a white Cadillac Escalade her dear friend Liz had purchased the year before, out of spite towards her second ex-husband. From outside her bedroom window Ily could hear the muffled beat to the song, "Halleluiah It's Raining Men," thumping from the subwoofers; Liz's all-time favorite tune.

The horn bellowed again, this time followed by a holler to, "Giddy up Girl! Get your ass in gear or we'll miss our flight!"

Ily smiled at the familiar voice. It was her adoring and sometimes psychotic friend, Hatti, who was also waiting impatiently in the driveway. Ily took one last look around the dimly lit bedroom to make sure the flat iron was turned off and she had grabbed the last of her beauty essentials from her vanity.

"This could be a crazy weekend," she said out loud.

Flying out the front door, carry-on luggage in hand, Ily was greeted by warm, welcoming smiles from her friends. Liz, Kate and Hatti anxiously awaited departure for the four women's first annual Las Vegas vacation.

Struggling down the front stairs with her baggage, Ily yelled, "Pop the trunk. Let's go!"

Within seconds she was in the back seat of the Caddy dishing out hugs and kisses to her friends. Liz threw the car in reverse, cranked the radio up to max volume, and headed towards the airport.

Outside a light snow began to fall with temperatures sitting around 36 degrees, making the Nevada desert heat that much more desirable. In the front seat Liz and Hatti carried on a conversation without even noticing the weather. Ily was in the back seat thinking about the fresh fallen snow and how pretty it was. She despised the cold, hard winters, but appreciated the first snow fall. Kate was quietly looking out the window, seated next to Ily, just happy to be leaving town for a few days. Their women's vacation seemed to have been forever in the making, and now the time was here allowing them to escape their lives for a while.

Once at the airport, Liz rounded the corners of the parking lot at excessive speed, found an open stall, and threw the car into park. She jumped out, ran to the back, and began unloading luggage. Ily hopped out of the backseat anxious to check in. Hatti exited the passenger door, pretending to vomit because of Liz's obnoxious driving. Kate exited the rear seat, stretched, and took note of where they had parked for when they returned.

"Did you guys notice where we parked?" asked Kate, surprised Liz didn't notice.

Liz peered around the back of the Cadillac, read the sign in front of her out loud, and immediately began throwing the luggage back into the vehicle.

"What in the world are you doing?" Hatti questioned.

"Did you see where we parked?" Liz shouted, back at Hatti.

They all turned to read the sign, indicating they were parked in stall number 66, row C. No one knew what Liz was in such a tizzy about. This spot seemed just fine to them.

"*Sixty-six*? That is the sign of the devil!" Liz exclaimed, "I am not getting on an airplane knowing we are parked in row C, stall 66."

Ily argued with her, noting the Devil's sign as 666 and parking in spot 66 meant nothing. The fight was not worth the energy, so they piled back into the vehicle and moved about the parking lot, once more, seeking another parking stall.

Liz found a location closer to the door, so her impulse move was quickly forgotten and the women were back on track. They unloaded the luggage for the second time, grabbed their hand bags and Kate wrote down; row D, stall number 17. The wheels on their luggage made tracks in the snow as they maneuvered to the airport entrance.

Ily and Kate led the way inside, with Liz and Hatti close on their heels. At the counter, a middle aged woman of average height, hair tied back in a tight pug, and very little makeup, smiled at the foursome and began giving her opening line with pride.

"On behalf of Allegiant Air, good afternoon and welcome to Outagamie County Airport. Will the four of you be traveling together today?" asked the plain, but cheerful woman.

"Of course we are! These are my girls!" shouted Liz, drawing attention to herself.

"We're headed to Vegas, baby!" cackled Hatti.

The attendant gave a knowing smile, printed boarding passes for all four women and wished them a safe flight and big winnings.

They had plenty of time before boarding the plane and decided to grab a scone and cup of coffee from the small café. They wanted to have something in their stomachs before the four hour flight. The scones tasted good and the coffee warmed them from the walk inside, through the snow.

"I have to stop and use the Little Ladies room before we go through security or I will piss my pants during the full body search," proclaimed Liz.

"No problem, girlfriend. We will grab a drink at the bar and you can meet up with us there," volunteered Hatti. She grabbed hold of Liz's carry-on suitcase, which definitely exceeded all size and weight limits.

Hatti, Kate, and Ily wandered over to the bar and grill, found a table, and ordered a round of drinks. Kate proposed a toast to the first annual girls' get-away. When Liz returned from the restroom, she ordered her drink and the four women relaxed, comfortably bantering, teasing, and talking smart in the airport lounge.

Forty-five minutes later, Ily, Hatti, Kate, and Liz made their way out of the bar and into the security line. Liz realized her boarding pass and driver's license were nowhere to be found. She racked her brain trying desperately to recall where she had left them.

"Shit! Ily, where the hell did I lose the damn thing?" Liz asked.

Over the loudspeaker an obviously annoyed voice paged Liz.

"Would Elizabeth Smith please report to the Allegiant Air counter for lost and found? Again, Elizabeth Smith please report to the counter immediately," pleaded the muffled voice.

The four women looked at one another and began laughing hysterically when they realized that on Liz's pit stop to the ladies room she had left her boarding pass and driver's license on the back of the toilet tank. They had been in the bar, passing the time and enjoying drinks, while missing every page for the past hour. Liz's lost - and now found - boarding pass, was awaiting pick up. She whirled 180 degrees on her heel and took off running for the check-in counter.

After retrieving her documents, security ensured she was selected for advanced search and questioning. In the moment

Liz acted as though she were a movie star being released from prison and blew kisses as she passed through.

"Good-bye, my good people of the airport," she shouted, waving.

"I hope you enjoyed searching me as much as I enjoyed you," she proclaimed, winking at the overweight security guard holding a wand in his right hand and waving to Liz with the left.

On the other side of surveillance Hatti, Kate, and Ily sat patiently waiting for Liz to be granted permission to join her friends once again.

"She makes sure everyone around knows when she is coming and going, doesn't she," questioned Kate, in a whisper.

"That's why we love her," Hatti reminded them, laughing.

Situated at Gate C, the four women discussed what they wanted to see, the things they wanted to do, and places they should go, upon arrival in Sin City. Ily was the typical party planner and had just about every minute of the trip arranged. Hatti let Ily have it about scheduling every minute of every God given day for them and ensured her friends this was her vacation to relax.

"All of your bickering is giving me a headache. Hatti, stop blubbering and Ily lay off the details. You really need to learn how to relax," Kate concluded, digging through her purse for aspirin.

She removed a large, white bottle, unscrewed the top, and poured an assortment of colored pills into the palm of her hand. There were small pills, white pills, round, red pills, and large, orange colored pills. She sifted through the myriad in her hand until she found an odd looking pill and asked Ily if it looked like Ibuprofen.

"Jesus, Kate! You are a walking pharmacy! How do you even know which pill does what?" asked Ily.

Kate laughed, looking at the bottle, and explained that she consolidated the pills into one bottle so she did not have to travel with seven different small bottles. Her explanation sounded legit. The two women began picking up pills trying to decipher the lettering on each. Ily found one odd duck in the bunch and asked aloud if it was a Roofie.

Just as she said the name of the date rape drug an officer passing by scurried over to where the four women sat. He stood bewildered, inches from Kate, who had a palm full of pills and an unlabeled pill bottle in her the other hand.

"What's going on here?" he asked sternly.

This guy obviously did not find Kate's pharmacy in her hand funny. They explained the rationale behind combining her pills into one bottle and insisted they were simply looking for aspirin. The airport security officer took a few pills from Kate's hand and began examining them. He knew the green one was for high blood pressure that Kate explained was because of her family. He thought the large, burnt orange pill was a multi-vitamin, and Kate agreed. Ily was not convinced this guy was legit, so she dug in, pulled out a pill, and asked the officer what the little blue one was for.

Everyone sitting around them laughed, having heard Ily's question. It was obvious this officer had not been laid in a long time, if ever. He then explained to Kate that it is important, especially when traveling, to keep your prescriptions separate for security reasons.

"Ok, ok…" she mumbled, barely acknowledging he was speaking.

Kate was busy dumping the pills from her hand into Ily's hand and digging through her purse for her cell phone.

"Dammit," she yelled, as her purse and all of the contents fell onto the floor.

Her friends bent to help reclaim the contents. Liz picked up a single pack of No-doze capsules, then another, and another, and another.

"What the hell do you have so many individual packages of No-doze for?" Liz questioned.

Kate thought it would be good to have just in case someone was tired and needed help staying awake to party. She explained that she cannot stay up past 11 p.m. most of the time.

Their airport security friend did not know what to say. The scene before him was beyond anything the technical school had taught him about his job. When the four women were seated back in their chairs, and Kate's purse was pulled back together, he looked at each of them and recommended calling the phone number on the bottle for assistance in clarifying what each pill was for.

Ily was already on Kate's cell phone dialing the 1-800-pills number on the back of the bottle. She looked at the officer and thanked him for his time, stating he could move along now.

"I am sure there are bigger and better crimes for you to be fighting here at the Outagamie County Airport," Ily stated sarcastically.

She was being extremely cynical; however, the officer found this comment fitting and turned to walk away.

He wished them well, tipped his hat and said, "Be safe ladies."

CHAPTER 2

Once the plane was safely in the air the women kicked back and began to relax. All four women needed this vacation and the time together. Their daily lives were consumed by work, family, and running a household. Their daily routine allowed very little time to play. Kate proved her point of a much deserved women's weekend as she began telling her story of a special trip the night before to the supermarket for coleslaw. Her husband didn't have a thing to bring to the company picnic while she was out of town.

Between homework with her children, packing, and cleaning the house, Kate made a special trip to the supermarket for her husband. Rather than going and taking care of business for himself, he moved around the house whining about how Kate gets a vacation, his children don't respect him, and he made up his mind that he was just not going to attend Corporate's picnic.

At 10:30 p.m., Kate arrived home, coleslaw in hand, and took a phone call while her daughter carried in the groceries. Kate was pleased her teenage daughter was doing something around the house, but later discovered a problem occurred when she failed to put the bag with the coleslaw in the refrigerator.

Kate's husband stormed through the house that morning complaining, once again, about how Kate gets a vacation and he was going to be late for work because he had to stop at the market for coleslaw.

When Kate's husband entered the shower, she and her daughter retraced their steps from the night before and found the bag with the coleslaw tucked away in a corner near the coffee pot and toaster.

"He is so screwed," Kate said, to her daughter, giving her a kiss, exiting the house and getting into Liz's Escalade.

To make a point Kate had left the coleslaw with a note for her husband that read,

Dearest Husband/Father, we forgive you for ranting and raving through the house the past 24 hours, shouting obscenities and accusing us of not loving you. Here is the coleslaw you ordered to prove we didn't neglect your needs for today's company picnic. We located the missing coleslaw hanging around the coffee pot and mingling with the toaster on the countertop all night. Enjoy your time alone.

Lots of Love,

Your fully supportive family

On the plane, Kate replayed the voicemail from her husband thanking her for picking up the coleslaw, and then with a laugh and light heartedness he proclaimed, "I love you and you are all a bunch of fuckers."

Kate found this so humorous she played the phone message over and over again for her friends. The corner of Ily's mouth turned up, revealing her big, beautiful, white smile and a twinkle in her eye. She mocked the message, letting her friends know she loved them and thought they were all a bunch of fuckers.

Laughter from the four women could be heard over the roar of the engines. Passengers seated seven rows back woke up, sat tall, and wanted to know what all the fuss was about. The damage was done. The unofficial exclamation for the weekend was locked in and ready to be thrown out at any time.

An hour into the flight, restless Ily was getting antsy in her seat.

"I'm bored, let's play Apples to Apples!" she suggested.

Hatti opened her eyes and mid-yawn asked, "Can't you just sit still for two minutes? I am not vacationing with you anymore. You can never just sit still. Besides, who brings a board game to Vegas?"

Ily spoke up for herself, "I do! It will be fun, come on!"

Liz indicated the need to use the airplane restroom again before they began the game.

"Didn't you go like an hour ago?" Kate remarked, teasing her about urinating more often than a 90 year old woman.

Kate offered to purchase Liz a pack of Depends once they landed. Liz stuck out her tongue, made her way to the restroom, and was back in a jiffy.

"That feels better," Liz informed her friends, with a sigh of relief.

She moved forward to take her seat and rapped her forehead on the overhead compartment with a loud thump. The noise from the impact caused people to look around. There stood Liz in a haze, holding her forehead. A man several rows back burst into laughter, having witnessed her ricochet off the overhead bin, and a stewardess came running up the aisle to see if she was ok.

Once all four women were safely seated again they ordered double shots of Skyy vodka and orange juice from the stewardess, who was also kind enough to bring Liz an icepack for the goose egg forming on her head. They toasted to a fun and fabulous vacation.

"To hell with men!" yelled Liz. "I haven't been laid in six weeks. There must be cobwebs forming by now!"

Hatti seconded her thoughts as they clinked together their plastic glasses.

"Let's make a pact right here, right now," Ily suggested.

"I pledge to be classy, sassy, and fun. I will make the most of my Vegas time and tease the hell out of all male slime!" she shouted with strength in her voice.

"Cheers!" they yelled, in sync.

"Let's make some memories," Kate concluded, snapping a picture of them taking a shot straight from the mini bottles of vodka.

Minutes later the four women found themselves in a heated game of Apples to Apples. Kate dealt the cards and read the first round of responses.

After about 30 minutes of hysterical belly laughing and continued ludicrous responses the flight attendant approached with a sour look on her face.

"I am sorry, but you are going to have to put the game away. Not everyone is having as much fun as you are," she stated, scornfully.

Ily, who never misses a beat when in the face of confrontation, immediately looked up and interjected. "Oh we're sorry, we thought this plane was going to Las Vegas, where fun is around every corner, where adults come to play; the city that never sleeps. Other passengers are welcome to play if they are feeling a little left out on a good time."

The attendant pursed her lips together, pulled up her skirt, and peered at the four smirking women. She stormed off toward the back of the plane and did not bother with them any further. The next few rounds were played a bit quieter out of respect for those seated around them.

"Honestly," said Kate.

"What are they going to do? Spontaneously land the plane to abort passengers due to a rowdy game of Apples to Apples!"

The plane touched down at McCarran airport about four o'clock. Liz, Kate, Hatti, and Ily were ready to take on the town and all that Vegas had to offer. Hatti, having lived in a large city as a college student, was used to hailing cabs. She whistled into the street bringing Yasser and his six-passenger taxi-van to an abrupt halt, curbside. Hatti crawled into the back of the van, while the other three women fought for the middle bench. Liz lost the war on seating and was forced into the passenger seat next to Yasser. She realized the ride was going to be all but dull when Yasser began adjusting the rearview mirror to reflect her breasts. He peered over at Liz's legs, extending long and lean from her Daisy Duke shorts.

The entire ride Yasser was rambling on heatedly about some water pollution crisis on the strip when Liz noticed his left hand was missing from the wheel and strategically placed down the front of his pants.

"What the hell are you doing!" she yelled.

The cab driver removed his hand from his pants and grabbed his camera, asking if he could take pictures of Liz's legs.

Oblivious to the obscenities taking place in the front seat, Ily spoke up. "You sure can! Just look at those long, strong thighs. Thoroughbred, I'd say. Snap away, baby, it's Vegas!"

Liz turned over her left shoulder and scowled at Ily in the back seat. Yasser was definitely aroused by the thought of snapping pictures of her soft skin thigh high, but wasn't getting a favorable reaction from Liz in the front seat. He didn't seem too bothered by the idea that he insulted any of them so he pulled out a joint, lit the end, and pulled long and hard, making the paper burn back rapidly.

"Want a toke," he asked casually.

The four women just stared at one another, not knowing if they were awake or dreaming this extraordinary nightmare.

Yasser spoke, quoting Ily from moments ago, "Relax, baby, it's Vegas!"

The taxi cab rolled to a screeching halt in front of Harrah's casino and the four women poured out of the door before the valet reached them. Ily threw enough money to cover the fare at him and some napkins at the people waiting in the cab line.

"Better wipe the seats first," she advised.

They snatched up their suitcases and hustled through the revolving entrance door of Harrah's Casino and Hotel. The sound of slot machines rang through the air and lights flickered and flashed. People from all walks of life passed-by. Hatti, Kate, Liz, and Ily stood taking it all in.

Off to the right was a well-dressed businessman perched upon a luxurious armchair. He was taking in the sights and sounds, while an older gentleman shined his shoes. To the left, hotel staff anxiously awaited guests to register and see that their needs were met. Ily made her way to the counter while Hatti, Liz, and Kate stood outside the VIP check-in. Ily provided her information to the concierge and received a packet containing a map of the casino, player point cards, and an assortment of coupons for entertainment at any one of Harrah's fine eateries, shows and clubs. Four room keys were provided and the concierge stated more could be made if necessary.

Ily walked back to the other women just in time to catch Liz saying, "Ok, we will see you tomorrow at the pool."

"Who was that?" asked Ily, with a look of interest.

"We made friends while you were checking us in. They have a cabana at the pool so we are all hooked up for tomorrow," Liz explained.

"Isn't it great to have big boobs?" she laughed.

The four women made their way to Carnival Tower, stepped onto the elevator, and rode to the 23rd floor. When the doors parted they were facing a bright orange wall with eclectic wall hangings, bright orange-multicolored carpeting, and a view of the strip through a window at the end of the hall.

"Room 2310, here we are," said Ily, leading the way. She inserted her key card and held the door open for Kate, Hatti, and Liz to enter the room.

"Whoa! They are definitely not afraid of color here are they?" exclaimed Kate.

It took a moment for their eyes to adjust to the bright colors in the room. The bedspreads were a floral print in purple, yellow, and red. The walls were a light orange and throw pillows in every shade of the rainbow accented the beds and chair.

Ily pushed in past Kate, leaving her luggage in the entryway, to jump on the beds.

Liz found a counter bolted to the wall on the right side of the room, opposite the bathroom. She flung her suitcase on top and within a blink of an eye the countertop smashed to the ground, landing at Liz's feet.

"Holy shit! I guess I packed one too many pair of shoes!" she exclaimed.

Kate took hold of Ily's bag for her, bringing their belongings into the room. She claimed stakes on the table and chair in front of the window. Ily sprang from the first bed to the second, flipped to the floor, grabbed her suitcase from Kate, and placed her bag in the corner of the room across from the mini bar. Hatti chose to unpack her belongings on top the large, fruit-orange-color faux leather bench at the foot of the bed.

Ily knelt down on the floor to unpack. She looked up at Kate and asked, "Is the floor wet over by you?"

Kate slipped her foot out of her sandal and stepped down on the soggy carpet, watching water squish between her toes. Ily stood to reveal the knees of her Capri pants and large, round water marks.

"It's like a bog over here," noted Kate. She continued to move a step to the right and left. "And over here and here and here…" she went on saying.

Liz stepped in front of the mini bar. Hatti pulled the unit away from the wall and gasped when she uncovered a stagnant pool of water hovering on top the carpeting.

"Sure 'nuf, the mini bar sprang a leak!" exclaimed Hatti.

"I think we should save what we can," Ily said, touching each item in the refrigerator to determine if the beer, wine, and individual liquor bottles were still cold.

"You never leave a good soldier behind," proclaimed Ily, unplugging the mini bar.

She loaded her arms full of the contents from the fridge and headed for the bathroom. "Liz and Kate, go down the hall and fill the garbage cans with ice. Hatti, you can
help me carry the booze to the bathroom. We'll ice it in the tub for later."

Once the contents from the mini bar were nestled nicely in the tub and covered with ice, Kate flipped the switch on the bright purple Mardi Gras mask lamp that sat on the nightstand, between the two double beds. She flipped the switch once; nothing. She flipped the switch again. Sparks flew, the bulb burst, and Kate let out a loud, shrill scream.

In the midst of chaos, Liz was attempting to plug her cell phone into the bathroom outlet and realized either Kate blew a circuit, or there was no power in the bathroom. Either way it was another item to add to the list of crazy happenings thus far. The missing boarding pass, the pill incident with the police, a rowdy game of Apples to Apples, the crazy cab driver who masturbates and smokes marijuana, and now the misfit hotel room; do they dare question what would be next?

It was all so ironic and funny that the women had not stopped laughing since they'd left home that morning. The four women decided this was not going to keep them down. Liz flung open the curtains in their room to reveal an amazing view of the strip, the lights, and all the glory Las Vegas had to offer.

Hatti appeared from the bathroom carrying four double shots of Jack Daniels and toasted to a memorable trip, thus far, and to many memories yet to be made.

"Cheers!" they shouted, throwing their heads back and slamming the shots.

CHAPTER 3

Toby Keith's Bar and Grill on the second floor of Harrah's was the hot spot for a quick meal, country music, live bands, and drinks. The concierge told them it was an all-around good place for good friends to start out the evening.

Liz is as large hearted and naive as they came. On the way into Toby's bar she stopped a black woman, dressed for success and absolutely flawless, to pay her a compliment.

"You are a very beautiful negro woman," Liz said, with a smile on her face and admiration in her tone.

The other three women could not believe the term Liz had just used to reference this woman.

"Oh shit! She didn't say what I think she said, did she?" asked Hatti.

Kate was speechless trying to pull her jaw up off the floor, so Ily spoke up before a fist fight broke loose.

Ily introduced herself to the woman, who was anything but flattered, and blatantly stated, "Please forgive our friend, she doesn't know her head from her ass. I believe what she meant to say is, dang girl, you look good! She told me she finds your beauty irresistible, your composure remarkable, and that you appear to be extremely forgiving of those that are ignorant."

The woman turned to Liz, smiled broadly, and gave her a hug.

Then she said, "Girl you a fine looking white woman yourself! My name is Jessica and I am one of many fabulous casino hosts here at Harrah's. You ladies enjoy your stay and good luck."

Jessica walked away while Kate, Hatti, and Ily smacked Liz out of sheer embarrassment.

"Next time you are going to say something stupid, run it by me first!" Ily ordered, laughing.

Their smiles stretched ear to ear and the glow that encompassed the four women as they made their way through the bar caught the attention of everyone present. Ily's spectacular figure, long auburn hair and expressive green eyes made heads turn everywhere she went. Her spunky personality made her not only nice to look at, but also a joy to be around. This evening she was wearing a black open back shirt, and in hot pink lettering read, *Flat Broke but Fun and Fabulous*.

Liz entered closely behind, walking with a spring in her step. She was sporting a red halter top and denim skirt accentuating her long, lean legs. Across her double D breasts were the words, *Whatever Floats Your Boat*. Enticed on-lookers made the statement dirty in their own minds, which was right up Liz's alley. She fluttered her eyes at single men, married men, old men and young men. It was what she did and what made her fun.

Kate rounded the corner and strolled into Toby Keith's bar with a ready for action look about her. She is a happy-go-lucky woman, with a bleach blonde pixie haircut, framing her round face and accentuating her bright blue eyes. She was wearing a hot pink tube top proclaiming, *Show me your*, on the front side, and *Money*, printed on the backside. Kate's outfit was complimented with black Capri pants that made her appear taller than usual. She clapped her hands in rhythm with the music, happy to be on vacation with her friends.

Hatti entered Toby Keith's bar last, but definitely made it clear that she was not least of the ladies. She was singing along to the hit country song, "When the Sun Goes Down," by Kenny Chesney. Hatti's attire for the evening was a crimson tube top full of sparkly black music notes, and printed on the front were the words, *Make Me Sing*. Hatti's strawberry blonde hair and blue-green eyes drew attention to her, but her voice was definitely her best asset. People turned to see which celebrity was singing along to the tunes as she strolled through Toby's close behind her friends.

The bar was full of folks enjoying a sit down dinner and country music. On the far side of the bar was a stage that extended the width of the room. The four women chose a round, black pub table with high back chairs off to the left. They reviewed the drink menu and mulled over the options for the evening. They discussed what they would like to do, see, and places to go once they had dinner.

At the table behind them a group of women laughed and chatted casually. At the bar a dozen or so men and women sat sipping drinks, minding their own business. At the end of the bar stood four men dressed in business suits, having what appeared to be an in-depth conversation, most likely about the day's events in the office. Ily thought the men to be stuffy and too intense for a fun bar like Toby's.

A nearly naked young lady in her early twenties approached the table, placing coasters in front of everyone.

In a bubbly voice she said, "Welcome to Toby's. What can I get for you ladies?"

Ily spoke up before her friends could say a word and ordered a round of lemon drop martinis in a tub for the four of them.

"Would you like to order food," asked the waitress.

The four women could not help but stare at her young, perky breasts bulging from her tight fitting top.

"Sure," said Hatti, "But we need a few more minutes to enjoy our drinks and look over the menu."

"Not a problem," said the spunky waitress, as she fluttered off to the next table.

Within minutes she was back carrying a tray with shots. She lined them up in front of each of the four women.

"One bourbon, one scotch, and one beer. The men at the bar to your left said they thoroughly enjoyed watching each of you walk in and believe you to be a fun group so they bought a round of our house shot as a token of gratitude."

Kate, Liz, Hatti, and Ily turned and leaned in close to one another giving a wink, a wave, and a kiss blown their way. Their admirers from a distance raised their glass and toasted from across the room as the women tipped their heads back, sucking down all three shots.

The night was starting off right and they continued to gab and sing along to familiar songs. Soon they began feeling very relaxed as the alcohol worked its magic. Ily's stomach rumbled and she knew if they didn't eat soon it would be an early night for them all. The cocktail waitress that had been serving them was now frantically trying to keep up as more people filed into the bar.

"I'm going up to the bar to order another round of lemon drop martinis and see if we can order food now. If the waitress comes by, flag her down. I need to eat," Ily told her friends.

She sprang from her bar stool and pranced to the bar, smiling and casting a sultry look at people as she passed by. When Ily reached the bar a tall, tanned, young stallion greeted her with a wink and smile.

"My name's Charlie, what can I get for you, beautiful?" he asked.

His eyes were like melted chocolate with lashes that never seemed to end. His body was tall, lean, and muscular, making him appear to be a perfect specimen. Ily's stomach fluttered, leaving her momentarily speechless.

"Ah, umm, four lemon drop martinis in a tub please, and we would like to order food too," she replied, feeling a bit tongue tied.

"Coming right up," said Charlie, turning around and reaching for a bottle of booze off the shelf.

His tight ass was amazing beneath his jeans. He turned back around just in time to catch Ily's eyes examining his backside.

"Wanna touch it?" Charlie asked, shaking his hips.

Ily turned bright red out of sheer embarrassment for staring at someone that was much too young for her.

"I, I, what? No, I don't want to touch it!" she exclaimed, feeling the heat in her cheeks.

Charlie laughed and continued making their drinks. Ily felt a spark of sassiness come over her. She pushed up on her tip toes, leaned over the bar closer to Charlie and said, "I was just amazed that you are as good coming as you are going!"

This time Charlie was the one who was stunned. He liked Ily's wit and confidence.

"Play your cards right, pretty lady, and you will see me cuming and going again yet tonight!" Charlie countered.

"Where are you from," Charlie asked.

"Wisconsin," Ily replied.

"Well, they sure know how to grow 'em in Wisconsin!"

A man's deep voice sounded from over Ily's right shoulder, startling her, and bringing her back to reality. She turned around and came face to face with the group of men in business suits she recognized from earlier that evening.

"Hello," he sang, in a sultry tone.

His voice caused her to turn her attention away from Charlie behind the bar. He was a man with strength, stamina and an ego to match. He and the other men stared at Ily as if waiting for her to speak.

"I'm sorry for interrupting. I thought you were speaking to me," stated Ily.

"We weren't speaking to you, but rather about you and your group of friends." he stated. "You all seem to be enjoying yourselves this evening. My name is Nolan. I am the General Manager of this casino."

As he spoke his chiseled jowls made Ily think of a bull dog. Nolan appeared to be in his 40's. He was graying at the temples and had steel eyes. He looked handsome and extremely professional in his navy blue suit and matching pink and blue tie. Nolan looked Ily square in the eye when he spoke. She found him intimidating, something that was rarely felt by Ily. In her mind she thought it a challenge to try to break him down. Ily and Nolan shook hands.

"It is a pleasure to meet you. We arrived today and certainly are enjoying ourselves," Ily informed the group of men, who continued to eye fuck her as she stood there.

"Here are your menus and drinks, gorgeous," said Charlie.

Ily turned back toward the bar, rolled her eyes at Charlie, grabbed the drinks and menus, and excused herself from the conversation.

As she began walking back to the table, she faced the group of suits staring at her ass and said, "It was nice meeting you, enjoy your evening."

With a wink and half smile Nolan called after her, "Try the pulled pork sandwich. They're excellent."

"Thanks for the tip," Ily called over her shoulder, licking her lips.

Just as she reached the table with the menus and drinks the waitress was back to take their order.

"I don't know what I am hungry for," said Liz.

"Me either," stated Kate, looking to Hatti for suggestions.

"The guy at the bar recommended the pulled pork sandwich," Ily offered.

"That sounds awesome," said Liz.

Kate and Hatti nodded in agreement.

"We will have four pulled pork and coleslaw sandwiches with french fries," Hatti told the waitress. "And bill the good looking rich guys in suits over there."

Hatti waved at Nolan and his friends, blew them a kiss, and mumbled under her breath, "They're all a bunch of fuckers. They have no clue how badly I'd wreck 'em in the sack."

They laughed at Hatti's confidence in the bedroom and went on talking until their meal was served.

"Oh my God, that was unbelievably good!" Kate commented about their pulled pork sandwiches.

Over casual conversation and the remaining martinis, Ily shared with her friends who the men in business suits at the bar were.

"Shut up! That is the General Manager of Harrah's?" asked Liz.

"That's what he told me," said Ily, taking a drink of her martini.

She noticed the men casually look their way, smile, and go on talking amongst themselves.

Hatti suggested they all hit the dance floor to burn off dinner. The disc jockey was playing Alan Jackson's hit song, "Good Time," as they pounded out on the floor. They were having a wonderful time dancing, clapping, and singing along. The next song brought on a knee-slapping, foot-stomping good time.

"Cotton Eyed Joe," overwhelmed the crowd. The dance floor spilled over with people swinging each other about, arm-in-arm. When the song ended Ily and Liz walked off the dance floor, passing by Nolan and his cronies.

"Hey!" Liz shouted, stopping and smiling at all five men.

She looked Nolan up and down and in a somewhat slurred voice stated, "Ily tells me you are the GM of this hotel. Are you really the big nut around here?"

Nolan looked at Ily and she shrugged her shoulders in a response that indicated she did not know where on Earth Liz got her information from.

"Yes, I am. And you are?" he replied courteously, shaking her hand.

"Liz. Liz from Wisconsin and this is my best girl, Ily."

Nolan was very amused by Liz and her powerful handshake.

"Yes, Ily and I have met but I hadn't caught her name until now," Nolan replied, cracking a cocky smile at Ily, now knowing her name.

There was a light in his eye that caught Ily's attention. She hadn't noticed this soft side of him earlier in the evening.

With enough lemon drop martinis in them all, Liz began telling the men of their adventures thus far and the mini bar disaster when they checked into their room. The other men gaped at Nolan who was stunned by Liz's description of the room.

"So we open the door to a very bright, but tastefully decorated room in all shades of orange. Ily took the far corner of the room and Kate put her bags on the table next to Ily. I found a countertop that thankfully was dead bolted to the wall and threw my suitcase on it. Wouldn't you believe it, the damn countertop crashed to the ground, leaving my items strewn about the room. Hatti made her home on the leather bench at the foot of the bed. All was going well until Ily stood up with wet pants, and it wasn't because she was horny," Liz recalled for the men.

Ily chimed in, "Kate squished enough water between her toes from the carpet to deem our room a wetland preserve. The carpet was so drenched that there are mushrooms growing in the corner!"

Nolan looked absolutely mortified. Liz continued telling the group of men how the light blew out and the room nearly started on fire from the sparks. As they talked the story grew even further from the truth.

"It was a good thing everything in the room was wet and that there was a loss of power in the bathroom or we would be toast!" cried Liz.

Kate and Ily told the men not to worry because the mini bar contents were on ice in the tub and the air conditioner's fan would help dry the carpeting.

The horror on Nolan's face could only be described as equal to finding a bloody, naked, dead body in your bed. He was cringing at the thought of clients in his hotel having encountered such a fiasco. Nolan pulled a pen from the breast pocket of his navy blue Armani suit coat and printed his cell phone number on the back of his business card.

"I apologize for the condition of your room and will personally see to it that the rest of your stay is a bit more enjoyable," stated Nolan.

He handed the business card with his cell phone number to Ily and another standard card to Liz.

Kate and Hatti had left the dance floor and now joined the conversation.

"Since you are feeling so awful about it you can buy the next round of martinis!" requested Hatti, pinching Nolan's butt.

Nolan ordered drinks for the four women and his group of friends. They all stood around chatting and learning more about one another. The evening continued with more lemon drop martinis, dancing, and friendships being made.

At one point during the evening the four women had turned their attention to the group of ladies that had been dining behind them. They were carrying on a conversation typical of women out for the night. It was a friendly chat regarding the need for time away from men and the benefits of belly laughing with girlfriends.

Kate turned to face the woman on her left side and shouted over the music, "Hey girlfriend, take that shit out of your ear so you can hear us!"

At that moment it seemed as if the record screeched, the room fell silent, and the spotlight focused on Kate.

Everyone at the table had a look of absolute shock.

Kate, oblivious to the damage her spoken words had caused, took another drink and then looked around at everyone's faces and asked, "What? What did I say?"

One of the larger women at the table spoke up.

"That shit in her ear is a hearing aid and in a noisy bar such as this she can't focus on the conversation. That is why she is not taking part in the conversation!"

Everyone began apologizing on Kate's behalf to the woman with the hearing aid. She did not seem to notice or care about what was obviously an honest mistake. The other women didn't seem to forgive and forget too quickly, so Kate apologized again for her stupidity and they moved on to another group of friendly souls.

The night went on and the drinks were strong. Kate took off Nolan's tie and wore it with pride wrapped around her forehead. Nolan jumped up on stage, grabbed the microphone, said something to the band and they began strumming, "Sweet Home Alabama," making the crowd go wild.

Ily joined Kate at the stage front and together they played the role of awestruck groupies. Liz and Hatti were perched on the bar, heads tilted back, while the bartender filled their mouths with a fruity concoction straight from the bottle.

About an hour later Nolan and his friends placed bets on Ily, proclaiming she would be puking by 11:00 p.m.

"I am from Wisconsin, you Ivy League asshole. I could drink you under the table!" Ily noted.

Nolan gave her a seductive look and commented, "I'd rather do something else with you *on* the table."

Ily snubbed his commentary by turning her back on him.

Liz stepped up in Ily's defense and began debating with Nolan about tolerance, size and holding your own when it comes to consuming alcohol. She told him they drank more than this on any occasion back home. Liz did not realize the toll all of the shots and lemon drops were having on Ily.

It all happened so quickly. She did not even have time to react. Ily knelt to the ground between two barstools and vomited. The people perched upon the stools casually glanced down at her limp body beneath them and continued on with their conversation.

Kate and Hatti emerged from the dance floor.

"Hey, where is Ily?" they questioned.

The man and woman at the bar pointed downward at the back of Ily's head. Liz flung herself to the ground next to Ily and pulled her hair back out of her face. Nolan whistled to the bartender, gave a signal, and security was there within seconds.

Apparently if you are highly intoxicated security shows up and kindly helps you back to your room. Liz assisted the two security officers, Cisco and Patrick, in lifting Ily off the floor of the bar. Each officer flung an arm around their shoulder and carried her out of the bar, to the elevators, and up to her room.

Kate found this to be quite hilarious and caught the moment on camera for a reminder to Ily in the morning. After all, that is what friends are for. She was like the paparazzi catching a celebrity on their way to rehab, snapping pictures of Ily with Cisco and Patrick. She even snapped a photo of Ily sporting Cisco's badge after she ripped it off his uniform, pinned it to her bra hanging out the top of her shirt and managed to slur out the question, "Is this a real badge?"

Hatti did her part as a dedicated friend and sang, "Na na na na, Na na na na, Hey, Hey, Hey, Good Bye," while waving her arms high in the air above her head.

"Peace out, girlfriend. See you in the morning," Kate called after Ily, turning to wink at Nolan.

He had won the bet. Ily would never hear the end of it. Cisco, Patrick, and Liz successfully tucked Ily into bed and returned to the bar. The excitement for the night was over. Liz joined up on the dance floor with Kate and Hatti for a few more hours of fun at Toby's.

CHAPTER 4

It was close to 4:00 a.m., when Liz, Kate, and Hatti headed back to the room to check on Ily, who they now referred to jokingly as, Sleeping Beauty. Nolan came up with that one.

The three drunken women entered the hotel room still reliving the evening play by play. Kate passed out mid-sentence on the bed adjacent to where Ily lay snoring. Hatti kicked off her shoes and headed to the bathroom, only to be shoved aside by Liz flying full speed towards the toilet. Liz was vomiting profusely while Hatti staggered around the room putting on her pajamas and eventually crawling into bed next to Kate.

Ily had gotten five hours of sleep and woke with a terrible hangover and excessive thirst. She grabbed a bucket and headed down the hall for more ice to eat and to keep the bathtub contents cool.

When she returned to the room, Ily noticed Liz was no longer in the bathroom. She had finished vomiting and crawled across the room to their bed. Ily thought a few more hours of sleep might kick her headache, so she lay down in bed and pulled the covers up over her shoulders. The room felt a bit cool, but her body felt as though she were overheating from alcohol withdrawals, so she snuggled in tighter.

Hatti was lying on the neighboring bed, snoring loudly. She still wore beads around her neck that were pathetically earned the night before. Kate lay sound asleep next to her. Ily leaned over to turn out the table lamp and took a second glance at Kate. Something was hanging from the side of her mouth.

Ily rolled out of bed and stepped closer to Kate. She picked the mystery item off her face. When Ily pulled, the mystery object just kept coming out from her mouth like something in a horror movie. Kate had rolled over in bed and puked down the side of the mattress while Ily was out getting ice. Hanging from the side of her face, Ily discovered a piece of the pulled pork from dinner.

"Disgusting," she said out loud, as she stood there laughing to herself and holding the foot-long, undigested piece of meat that obviously came all the way from Kate's intestines.

This was too good not to share, so she woke Hatti and Liz, told them the story about the puked up pulled pork and presented the evidence.

"Oh my God, that is sick," gagged Liz.

"Does she not chew her food?" questioned Hatti.

They took pictures of Kate and her infamous piece of pork. They held it inches from her face, laid the piece of meat on her pillow, and nestled it back on her cheek where Ily had found it. The three women laughed heartily at Kate's expense, while she purred on in her sleep like a kitten.

Ily almost forgot her head hurt and Hatti pissed her pants laughing so hard. When they had their fill of fun; Liz, Ily, and Hatti returned to bed. Kate was none the wiser, and slept until the sun came up over the Nevada desert that morning.

Ily was the first to rise and head for the bathroom. She flipped on the light and squinted to find her way to the toilet. A bit of vomit remained on the seat from Liz, the tub was still packed with ice and booze, and clothing lay strewn about the room. She was still groggy while seated on the toilet, but came to a bit when she noticed dried, crusty blood caked on her left leg.

Ily wiped the blood off but noticed more on her right leg. She began examining herself and what she found was not pretty.

There was blood splattered sporadically all over her body and clothing.

"What the fuck?" she asked herself, sitting there in the dimly lit bathroom.

Ily had no clue where all the blood came from. She was now wide eyed with horror.

She followed the trail of blood from her body, to the floor, and around the toilet. There were splotches of red blood on the tile, the carpet in the hallway, and over to the bed she had left only moments ago.

Bewildered, Ily pulled back the covers from where she had been laying and noticed more blood on the white bed linens.

"What are you doing and why are all the lights on?" Hatti asked, annoyed.

"There is blood everywhere and I am trying to figure out where it came from," Ily indicated.

Carefully pulling back the covers, she realized the bed linens were worse off than she was.

"Oh my God! Yuck!" Ily screamed.

Liz woke in a haze and rolled from her left side to her back to face Ily.

"You don't have underwear on?" she screamed at her friend.

"You slept with me all night long, farting, and you're not wearing underwear! Dear God, that is so gross!" Ily scolded Liz.

Now that Liz was awake she sat up in bed laughing at Ily's commentary.

"Why are we up so early, anyway, and where did all the blood come from?" Liz wanted to know.

Ily turned to her and yelled, "That's what I have been trying to figure out!"

Liz sat up in bed holding her head, peered through squinting eyes, and weakly whined to her friends, "My toe hurts."

She pulled her foot out from under the covers revealing her bare canvas vagina, blood crusted legs, and one fucked up big toe.

On her right foot the largest toe's nail stood straight up. The entire toe was swollen and covered in layers of old, dried blood.

"Hey!" exclaimed Kate, in her very high pitch, Wisconsin accent. "I remember that happening."

"You do?" questioned the other three women, in unison.

"Yeah, before Ily puked at Toby's Bar and Grill and was hauled off by Cisco and Patrick, she was dancing with the lesbian, who later threatened to kick Liz's ass but settled for her foot instead," Kate stated casually.

"Nolan offered you ice for your toe, but instead, you used it to seductively, caress your breasts and nipples for him," added Hatti, laughing.

Kate continued to tell the story as if it happened only moments ago. She told them Liz miraculously recovered as soon as she saw Nolan back up on stage singing and joined in as a proud groupie once again.

"Ok, hold up," said Ily. "Who are Cisco and Patrick?"

Hysterical laughing rang throughout the room.

"She doesn't even frickin' remember!" stated Liz in sheer disbelief.

Hatti, Liz, and Kate all tried to help with the recollection of the events that led up to security being called.

"Ily, you made a bet with Nolan and his buddies that you would be able to drink them under the table, called them Ivy League Assholes, and then fell to the floor puking!" exclaimed Liz.

Ily paused for a moment taking in all the details laid out before her.

"Ok, but that does not tell me who Cisco and Patrick are."

Kate spoke up between laughing and gasping for air.

"They are the two security guards that tenderly dragged you back to the room. You pulled off Patrick's badge and pinned it to your push-up bra. I thought you would have trouble recalling the festivities, so I snapped pictures of it all," Kate proudly explained, pulling out her camera for review.

Ily lay on the bed reviewing the pictures from the night before. More laughter and snorting from the four women took place while they watched Ily's vast array of facial expressions. She began to recall bits and pieces of the evening. The pictures were worth a thousand words.

Liz sat on the bed quivering as she tried to push her toenail back into place without cracking it further. At least for now the wound had clotted, preventing further blood spatter. Kate refrained from laughing long enough to continue her story of the busted up toenail saga. She recalled each moment in full detail, adding a bit of character.

"Liz and I were at the bar ordering a round of drinks when the tall, about 5'10", dishwater blonde, approached us and asked if Liz wanted to dance. She kindly told her no and the woman apologized, stating she didn't know Liz and I were together. We turned to face one another and laughed it off, going about our business," Kate explained.

"Five minutes later, there is Ily bumping and grinding with her on the dance floor!" recalled Liz.

Kate went on saying, "And then Liz screamed out, '*help, I need a man!*' To which every male in the place came running at us."

Liz explained it wasn't for her, but rather her friend, the sexy one, grinding with the lesbian on the dance floor. Even more men appeared out of the woodwork. Liz was laughing so hard she was crying and had difficulty telling Ily about the next part.

"So after rallying the troops of every good looking guy in the place, we selected and sent the dreamiest man out on the dance floor to rescue Ily from the alleged lesbian. Ily ends up telling him off and pushing him aside like yesterday's trash. We were standing back watching all of this go down in disbelief," Liz laughed hysterically.

Kate chimed in again, "Then, only moments later, Ily goes missing and vomits between two barstools occupied by a couple, so engrossed in conversation, they hardly knew she was there."

Nolan called for security to return her to our room and the dirty dancing lesbo returned for a second chance at love. Through clenched teeth Liz told her to find someone else's carpet to munch; she's not about to be no lesbo's brunch. Then the woman's fists clenched, her eyes went crossed, and she kicked Liz as hard as she could in the foot just before falling backwards and passing out, right before them.

"Liz, you said your foot hurt and went to sit with Nolan and his friends at the bar," added Hatti.

"Well that explains the throbbing pain I feel in my toe right now," said Liz, looking like freeze dried shit and covered in blood.

"And it also solves the mystery of where all the blood came from," said Ily, looking like she may throw up again.

Ily then turned to Liz begging and pleading, "Would you please just wear some underwear to bed next time I have to sleep with you?" It was more of a statement than question.

Liz and Ily were awestruck listening to Kate and Hatti relive the evening's events. Liz could barely remember her name this morning, much less details of what went on.

"Is it cold in here?" Kate asked, with a shiver.

"Yeah, aren't we in the middle of the desert? Why would it be so cold in our room?" Ily inquired.

Liz spoke up in a meek voice, hoarse from being hung over, dehydrated, and the second hand cigarette smoke she consumed.

"I turned the fan on yesterday before we left the room to help dry the carpet," Liz told them.

Hatti made her way over to the thermostat controls on the far wall. She hit a button to show the current settings. Her jaw dropped when she realized Liz's mistake.

"Oh fish balls!" she exclaimed. "No wonder we now have an ice rink instead of a bog on the floor and Kate's pulled pork puke is frozen midstream down the side of the bed! Liz, you idiot, you turned the fan *and* the air conditioning on high!"

The thermostat read 53 degrees. Ily was wrapped tightly in a blanket, Hatti played with the controls, and Kate used the hair dryer to warm her feet.

"Well, no wonder I did not have a hot flash all night," Liz confessed, trying to keep it light.

She was drilled by a series of pillows thrown at her from all corners of the room.

"It feels like a meat locker in here!" laughed Kate.

"My nipples could cut glass," exclaimed Hatti.

They laughed at her comparison, feeling their own nipples stiffen from the cold.

The vibrant orange room on the 23rd floor of Harrah's had once again come to life with laughter. The past 16 hours were amazingly fun, exciting and eventful. The incidents that occurred, the people they had met; it was a wonder they had all survived the night.

CHAPTER 5

"I don't feel so good," Liz whined.

She was pale in the face and had been dry-heaving all morning. Hatti grabbed the dry cleaning bag from the closet and instructed Liz to carry it with her just in case she needed to be sick. Once in the elevator, on their way downstairs, Liz began moaning, groaning, and gagging. She held the dry cleaning bag in front of her, belching and spitting into it. The doors on the elevator opened two floors beneath theirs.

The couple's smile faded as they looked at Liz.

She had tears in her eyes and shouted at them, "Don't come in here."

The doors closed and the elevator continued to move again. Ily, Hatti, and Kate laughed hysterically at Liz. She seemed to get increasingly sick with every floor they passed.

Liz's dry-heaving stopped and they ditched the bag in a laundry cart outside the elevator on the main floor. They headed toward the casino looking like the walking dead. All they wanted was to make it to the pool without vomiting. Liz's moans and groans of self-induced pain drew enough attention.

Once inside the casino, a short, stocky man with fair skin and goldenrod hair running the roulette table caught Ily's attention. He smiled as the four women approached.

"Pretty ladies, would you like to try your hand at roulette?" he called out to them.

The hair on his upper lip danced as he spoke.

Ily stopped, put her hand up and said to her friends, "Let's give our luck a try today."

Hatti was on a tight budget for this vacation and whined about not wanting to waste her dollars gambling.

"Yeah, let's save our money for drinks at the pool," Liz backed her up.

"I have a feeling about this. Everyone ante up $100. We are betting on red," Ily instructed.

"Why red?" questioned Kate, standing at the back of the group.

"Red. In honor of Rita. I think she has been keeping an eye on me," proclaimed Ily.

She was not a real religious person, but acknowledged believing in something, and that something was her recently deceased, Great Aunt Rita. This something was pulling her towards the man with a whimsical mustache and the need to gamble, and gamble big.

A bit reluctant and yet trusting in their beloved friend, each woman dug through her handbag, pulling out $100 each, and cautiously placed their money on red, for Rita Red. The croupier smiled, making his mustache move upward. With a twinkle in his eye he gave the wheel a spin and threw the tiny ball in the opposite direction.

The four women stood gripping one another's hands, anxiously watching the ball roll and tumble around the wheel, seeking to determine the fate of their impulse gamble. Tick, tick, tick, tick, tick was the only sound they heard in the entire casino. The wheel began to slow and the marble continued to toss about as if in slow motion.

Ily closed her eyes and tightened her grip on her friends' hands. Hatti and Kate looked from their money to the spinning wheel and back. Hatti wanted to pull her money off the table and hightail it out of the casino.

Liz continuously chanted "Come on, Rita Red, come on!"

The ball landed with a loud plunk in the slot labeled number five, red.

"Oh my God!" exclaimed Hatti and Kate, now showing signs of tears of joy.

Liz picked her jaw up off the table and Ily opened her eyes just in time to see the croupier put the glass marker on five, red.

"We won!" she exclaimed, "We really did it, you guys."

"Nice work Ily," emanated Liz, watching the mustached man distribute chips to the other players and finally getting around to their fair share of the dispersed winnings.

After high-fives were given and received from everyone around, who had gathered to see what the commotion was about, the lucky four took their winnings and walked away from the table.

"This is shaping up to be a hell of a day," noted Liz.

They were grinning ear to ear now. Passersby could not help but smile in their direction. The glow of a remarkable gamble and win was with them.

"Next stop: poolside lounging," proclaimed Ily.

The Harrah's pool was an Olympic size, rectangular shape, four feet deep all around. The parameter of the pool was well maintained shrubs, vibrant flowers, and a concrete patio, equipped with lawn chairs, beckoning sunbathers. To the left, pricey cabanas were furnished with ceiling fans, wicker patio sofas piled high with pillows, two end tables, and a personal attendant to cater to the lucky tenant's every need. Directly in front of the pool entrance, where the women stood taking it all in, was a tiki bar.

There were three middle-aged men belly-up at the bar drinking Heineken beers and talking amongst themselves. The tiki bar was staffed by a decent looking man in his mid-40's of average height, dark hair and the prominent beer belly evident of most men his age. The bartender busied himself filling stainless steel coolers with ice.

Liz led the way down the right side of the pool and selected four lounge chairs.

On the opposite side of the pool two young ladies in bikinis were sunbathing. A cocktail waitress in sneakers, bikini top, and skirt raced around carrying a bucket of bottled water and a platter of fresh fruit into one of the cabanas. She flipped a switch to activate the fan and with a pleased look, walked away to take drink orders from other pool-goers.

Seated comfortably a few chairs down from Ily was a man about her age sitting alone, quietly enjoying a breakfast sandwich from McDonald's.

"Hey," Ily called to him, "What'cha eatin'?"

The man raised his breakfast sandwich into the air and replied, "Grease to cure a hangover."

Ily lay on her side; legs elongated, and seductively asked, "How many do you have?"

He peered into the white paper bag, looked back up at her and gestured casually that he had two sandwiches. One he was devouring and the second remained in the bag.

"May I have one?" asked Ily, pushing her breasts closer together revealing amazing cleavage.

He seemed a bit flustered by her bold demeanor and request for his food, but shrugged his shoulders, reached into the bag and pulled out a grease-soaked wrapper containing the second breakfast sandwich.

"Thanks for sharing with me," Ily said seductively, with a wink.

She unwrapped the sandwich and took a huge bite.

"What the hell," Ily shouted. "Ham? Who orders ham? Next time you buy me a breakfast sandwich unknowingly, for the love of God order sausage!"

Ily smiled his way, blew him a kiss, and went back to her breakfast.

He returned the wink, apologized sarcastically for what was obviously an honest mistake, and returned to his solitude.

"Seriously, what was that?" Kate questioned, furiously. "If I would have asked him for a sandwich he would have told me to walk my fat ass to McDonald's and get my own food!"

Ily gave her a snotty look and popped the last bite of breakfast sandwich into her mouth.

The cocktail waitress had made her way over to them announcing Rum Runners were the drink special for the day.

"I don't drink rum," Hatti blatantly stated, with a sour look on her face.

"I don't know what a rum runner is but it sounds fab. I will take one Rum Runner," Ily ordered.

Liz and Kate stated, they too, would enjoy a Rum Runner drink special to start the day. Hatti, who proclaimed to not like rum, ordered a banana daiquiri. When the waitress left Ily looked at Hatti with a smirk on her face and said, "You do know daiquiris are made with rum."

"No they are not. It is banana liqueur," Hatti retorted.

"Really?" challenged Ily. "Ok, so we're in Vegas. Let's do something to settle this accordingly. I will bet your share, $100 we just won, that the banana daiquiri you ordered contains rum."

Kate sat quiet listening to the details of the bet. Eager to participate, Liz stood up on her lounge chair affirming she would conduct a poll.

"Excuse me everyone at the pool! Good morning! Hello! My friends are trying to settle a bet and we need your input. Please raise your hand if you believe banana daiquiris are made with rum," Liz quizzed the crowd.

The three men at the bar drinking Heinekens raised their beers to demonstrate their vote of confidence. The two women sunbathing raised their arms high in the air and the McDonald's man lifted his muscular arm in agreement, as well.

"Better get your wallet out," Liz teased Hatti.

She glared her eyes at Liz. "Not without further proof," she pressed.

Moments later, the pretty little cocktail waitress strutted over with a drink tray in hand. Three rum runners were distributed to Kate, Ily, and Liz.

"And a banana daiquiri made rum free just for you ma'am," she said, handing Hatti a tall frozen concoction.

"Ha! See, I told all you bitches. Rum Free!" retorted Hatti.

The cocktail waitress, somewhat shyly, set the record straight by adding, "Well, not really rum free but the bartender is sweet on you ma'am. He told me to tell you that your drink is whatever you want it to be; rum free or not."

Hatti looked like a love-struck teenager and her friends were laughing their asses off. The waitress continued to speak.

"Dave, the bartender, said the two of you would have a good time spending your friend's money later this evening," their poolside waitress said, with a knowing smile.

All four women looked over at the tiki bar. Dave was standing tall, waving their way, but seemed to only notice Hatti. His big brown eyes beneath dark lashes shone brightly against his tanned skin. At second glance, he was more handsome than Ily had originally thought.

Hatti's gaze penetrated him as they stood taking one another in. She raised her drink and seductively fumbled for the straw with her lips, never releasing her hold on him.

Kate leaned closer to Liz and asked if it had gotten hotter outside. Hatti mumbled something to her friends about her drink containing the best damn rum she had ever tasted and slowly wandered off in Dave's direction.

The other three women removed their clothing down to their bathing suits, applied sun screen and went to sit on the edge of the pool. They were peacefully enjoying their rum runners and taking in the scenery when Liz asked if Ily thought Hatti would really pay her the money they bet.

"I doubt it, but I will get it out of her somehow," Ily implied, laughing.

CHAPTER 6

More people arrived at the pool as the day went on. The temperature was a toasty 82 degrees, making the cold Wisconsin weather back home long forgotten. Hatti had rejoined the group, but not before getting bartender Dave's digits. She told her friends she had high hopes of connecting with him later in the day.

The four women made their way down into the water and were mingling with the diverse crowd that came to the pool to cool off. Most folks came and went, and others comfortably nested themselves on patio chairs, with iPods or reading material.

One woman claimed to be a friend of Britney Spears. She said she lived in Los Angeles and was spending the day at the pool with her daughter, while her semi-pro golfer husband, made his monetary value increase with each putt on the Nevada greens.

Then there was the black guy who swam past nonchalantly and said to the four women, "Hey sure is hot. How long have you been here?"

To which Kate replied, in a thick Wisconsin accent, "Oh, just a couple of days."

He looked over the group and smiled.

Mocking the Wisconsin accent he said, "Oh ya, I got here three days ago and I was a white guy!"

They all belly laughed at his joke and learned he was in Las Vegas with his sister and her husband, hoping to get lucky on the slots, and with a bit of luck, some hot slut.

Three rounds of rum runners and Dave's special daiquiris for Hatti had all four women buzzed, burnt, and yearning for more. They exited the pool to reapply sunscreen. The McDonald's man and Heineken boys were long gone and a new character had moved into their neighborhood at the pool.

Liz noticed him first and made the comment that he belonged with the Blue Man Group from The Venetian. His head was the size of a basketball, shaved clean. He was sporting bright blue, Ray-Ban eye goggles and his body obviously inflated complements of steroid injections. He watched them while they applied sunscreen to one another.

Fat head pulled his blue, Ray-Ban sunglasses down his pointed little nose and peered over the top. He licked his lips, indulging in the moment and spoke in a rather annoying tone.

"Mmmmm, I'd like some of that," he said.

Ily looked at him and cynically replied, "It's your wet dream; make it as big as you want."

They tried desperately to ignore him, but this guy's thick head just wasn't catching on. Ily rolled her eyes at her friends and lounged back comfortably in her chair. Kate hid beneath a large sun hat and glasses.

"My name is Tom," Fathead said abruptly.

He moved his chair closer to the four women. Tom continued speaking his practiced self-introduction.

"I own my own used car dealership. My guys who work for me are so good I don't have to be there, though. They work their asses off making money and I come out here to spend it," Tom blurted out.

The women threw looks back and forth, revealing anything but expressions of interest or the slightest hint of being impressed.

"Shouldn't you get back to the Venetian for the show tonight?" Hatti asked, snickering with her friends.

Tom was ignorant to the sarcasm in her tone and went on talking about himself for another 15 minutes. An eternity seemed to have passed before he stated the reason he wandered over in their direction.

"I saw you had sunscreen before," he implied, peering over the top of his blue Ray-Ban shades.

"Would one of you mind helping me put some on my head? Bald is beautiful, but I think I am beginning to burn."

Tom's head was as red as a raspberry. Liz volunteered enthusiastically. It was apparent that she drank enough for logic and reason to be dismissed. Liz whipped the sunscreen from her bag, applied a thick line down the front of her own body, and began rubbing herself against Tom in a seductive, circular motion.

Tom, the steroid inflated fathead, enjoyed this way too much. The three women laughed hysterically watching as his pinky finger size penis began to penetrate from the front of his swim trunks. Witnesses looked on in awe at the poolside seduction. Liz finished Tom off with the lotion by rubbing his bald head between her sweaty breasts.

"There! Now go away," Liz said, pushing him backwards.

"That was wild!" Tom exclaimed.

He was so riled up after that he talked about how big his dick is and even offered to show the four women a picture of it!

"No! Oh my word, we have experienced enough of you," Ily assured him.

Twenty minutes later, the after sex endorphins took over, and Tom fell asleep in the chair next to Kate. He continued to fry like bacon in the sun, snoring like a freight train. At one point he rolled over and flopped a thick sweaty arm across Kate's chest.

"Oh gross!" she cried, throwing his arm off of her, but it just flew back at her and landed hard against her chest with a loud smack.

"That is it!" she shouted. "I am going back in the pool."

Her friends laughed and Kate glared her eyes.

"You're all a bunch of fuckers!" she yelled, storming off toward the pool in her oversized sun hat. This just made her friends laugh even harder.

"Hey look who it is," said Liz, peering toward the entrance to the pool area.

Nolan, one of the men they had met the night before, strutted in wearing a white t-shirt and printed on the front was a slogan for In and Out Burgers. As he walked toward them his thigh muscles worked vigorously, bulging beneath his black running shorts. His sun bleached hair was still damp with sweat. He had been watching them from the second floor fitness center for the past hour or so, while executing his daily workout.

"Well, hello there," he spoke, in a deep voice.

"Who found this one," Nolan asked coyly, peering down at Tom who continued to snore on his lounge chair.

"He's a stray," explained Ily. "Liz seduced him with sunscreen, he came in his shorts, and then fell asleep."

Nolan raised an eyebrow, intrigued by the story.

"Lovely," he said, flashing a smile that made all four women's hearts pound.

Ily thought, "Boy this guy really thinks he is something special."

She turned to her friends for backing. This was far from what she discovered. Hatti, Liz and Kate stood in awe of Nolan's presence and reveled in the fact that he not only remembered their names, but had made a concerted effort to visit them at the pool.

"Has your room situation been taken care of to your liking?" Nolan asked.

Before the others could wipe the drool and close their mouths long enough to answer, Ily spoke up.

"We're doing fine, thank you."

Ily assumed Nolan threw his prestigious title, male authority, and money around more often than she could stand. Nolan seemed a perfectionist, or in Ily's mind, a high maintenance, male, pain in the ass. He had paid for drinks the night before, most likely hoping to take an intoxicated volunteer back to their room. He also had her hauled out of Toby Keith's bar, which pissed her off. She was harshly judging this man and knew it, but for some reason Nolan threatened Ily and that didn't sit well with her either.

Nolan respectfully offered to put the women up at Paris Casino for the duration of their stay. He was flexing his muscles and power in Vegas for the women again today. Hadn't he done enough?

"It's a lovely hotel and the rooms have recently been remodeled. I have friends over there who will take good care of you ladies," Nolan proposed.

"Wow, really? I have always wanted to see the casino and being able to stay there would be a dream come true!" Hatti exclaimed.

Liz accepted without so much as saying the words. She was awestruck by the luck they were continuously having.

Nolan looked to Kate and Ily for their two cents. They turned to Ily for her acceptance.

"Oh, please say yes Ily," Hatti begged, with a pleading look on her face.

Liz and Kate were so star struck by Nolan they would have slept in the alley if he told them that was best. Ily, a bit reluctant, accepted Nolan's room offer at Paris Casino.

Still, she could not help but wonder what this Ivy League showoff wanted from her and her friends. She did have to admit he seemed genuine, was extremely handsome, and, thus far, Nolan had treated them very well. Ily hoped his generosity was not a mask for any ill-intentions.

"My friends and I have had a lot of fun here at Harrah's, Nolan. We would love to experience another one of your casinos." She paused, and then continued speaking. "On one condition…"

Nolan raised his eyebrow this time in suspicion of her.

"Well now, this should be interesting," he teased.

Ily's blood was racing as her heart pounded beneath her barely there bathing suit.

"We would like you to join us for dinner and drinks this evening at the Range Steakhouse. You can tell us all about life in Nevada," proposed Ily.

Nolan would have loved to spend more time with the four women, especially Ily. He was taking a liking to her wit, charm, and sassiness with him. Most women obliged his every wish and she seemed to stand on her own two feet. He had always been attracted to strong women. Her confidence in any situation he had seen, thus far, was a tremendous testament to her character and a complete turn on.

"Dinner would be lovely indeed," replied Nolan, not allowing his stare to release Ily's eyes. "However, I have to work until around nine o'clock and then my children are expecting me home for ice cream sundaes and our favorite television show."

"*Uh huh,*" Ily thought. "*He's married and not telling them. Kids and a curfew, but no ring; what kind of fool did he take them for?*"

Nolan spoke to the other three women as well this time.

"Would it be safe to say we meet at Paris' Le Burger Brassiere tomorrow at a quarter past nine o'clock? We can see where the night goes from there," Nolan offered.

The four women nodded in agreement, feeling lighter than air at that moment. Nolan bid farewell and walked back out the door he had unexpectedly appeared from. While walking away, he thought to himself how beautiful each woman he just met with was. Most of all he could not keep his mind off Ily. There was something about her that made his heart pound. His arms wanted to reach for her and pull her close. Nolan knew he needed to be careful with Ily, though. He could tell she was a wild flower and yet guarded whenever he came around.

"He is incredibly good looking," Hatti commented, staring after him.

"Delicious," was all Liz could manage, licking her lips.

Ily tried to remain calm and inconspicuous, guarding her attraction to Nolan.

"Eww, he had nose hair popping out, sweaty balls, and besides, he is very self-consumed. Not to mention a bit older," Ily pointed out.

Liz commented on the size of his thigh muscles and then concluded that he was most likely trying to compensate for small family jewels between those thunderous thighs. Trying to find fault in Nolan was like searching for the proverbial needle in a haystack. Each woman tried to pick him apart out of sheer uncertainty as to who he truly was. It was their way of making heads or tails of this elite stranger who popped into their lives. Thus far, Nolan was every bit a gentleman, and professional in his demeanor.

"He wouldn't deserve you, Ily," said Kate, reading between the lines.

Ily turned toward her friend, stunned that anyone had read her thoughts.

"Ivy League asshole, to be sure," she stated, simply.

Kate decided not to press any further, although she thought Nolan charming, she knew he would break Ily's heart. Ily had been alone for quite some time and had not been on a date in only God knows how long. Ily gave all of herself to her work and her dog.

"Ily needs to find love with another human," Kate thought. *"But is Vegas the place to do so?"*

At that moment the burnt blob of shit, Tom, began to stir, making random grunting noises and stretching. He would be waking soon and the four women had made a plan to vanish before he woke. Acting quickly, all four women rounded up their belongings and frantically moved to a new neighborhood at the pool.

Once they were situated at a safe distance, the cocktail waitress appeared, took their drink orders, and this time they included a shot to toast a safe escape from Tom. They were going to celebrate their new friend, Nolan, the anticipation of Paris Casino, and the splendid time they were having in Vegas.

As the day progressed the sweltering sun continued to melt their minds and kiss their bodies. The four women talked with a vast array of people and told stories of their visit to the Nevada desert thus far. They held the attention of folks from all walks of life who were envious of the excitement the four women were experiencing.

"I'm hungry. As long as we have our belongings pulled together and our bathing suits are dry let's cross the strip and have lunch at Caesar's Palace," Ily suggested.

Liz, Kate, and Hatti agreed. Ily's idea sounded like a remarkable plan. The four women could use some time out of the sun and something solid in their stomachs. Each of them began dressing for the excursion to Caesar's Palace.

"I could go for some food, too," acknowledged Liz.

"Yeah, my belly is rumbling and it ain't because I gotta fart," announced Hatti.

"Well, I wouldn't think so since you passed gas all night," Kate retorted.

"I thought that was Liz, Ms. I don't wear underpants to bed!" shouted Ily, still grossed out by the thought of Liz's bare ass beneath the sheets.

The group of men who occupied the cabana, which was set up earlier that morning, cautiously eyed the four women. Throughout the day each of the men made random comments to catch the women's attention. Finally one of them admitted to recognizing Liz.

"Were you the girl outside the Diamond Lounge yesterday?" he asked.

Liz looked a bit shy and indicated she was; however, she couldn't remember his name.

The man extended his hand and said, "You're Hollywood, right?"

Liz was impressed he had remembered the fictitious name she had thrown out. She stood wide eyed and tongue tied.

"My friends call me Sparky. I would like it if you did the same," he confessed.

The four women now chatted with the five men from the cabana. They had overheard the jokes between the women and demanded to know which of them did not wear underwear to bed. Ily became impatient and attempted to round up her friends, who were now moving closer to the cabana and men, than the exit.

"Where are you ladies off to in such a hurry?" questioned Sparky.

Hungry and feisty Ily intercepted his question and fired back with, "Take off your pants and we'll tell you."

This brought the house down with hearty laughter from anyone within earshot. Kate was the first to regain composure and filled them in on lunch plans at The Forum Shops inside Caesars Palace.

"Come on along if you'd like," Liz invited.

Sparky looked at his friends who subtly nodded their heads no.

"I think we are pretty well set here in our cabana, but when you return hook back up with us," he concluded.

The four women waved goodbye to their new friends stating they would be back in a couple hours.

CHAPTER 7

While crossing The Strip to Caesars, they joked about all of the male piranhas at the pool that day. Kate found it amusing that men of all ethnicities came to check out Ily, and ironically, Nolan was the only white guy she shied away from! They continued to banter about Liz not wearing underwear, Ily puking at the bar, Kate's undigested pulled pork and Hatti's incessant snoring.

"This is just so much fun. Thank you for letting me be a part of all this," said Kate.

"Absolutely, monkey nut! Who would be our poopsie schmoopsie if you weren't here?" Hatti wondered aloud.

Ily and Liz rolled their eyes back in their heads. Her choice of words often times threw them for a loop.

Hatti laughed at her friend's teasing ways. She knew they loved each other very much and this weekend was an affirmation of their patience and devotion to a rock-solid friendship.

Seated at the table inside the café of Caesar's, Ily raised her glass in a toast to the first annual girls' vacation.

"A toast to my girls! May we always love one another, laugh with one another, and move through life with one another," she stated.

"Amen!" shouted Hatti.

"Cheers," smiled Liz, beaming with delight.

"You're all a bunch of fuckers!" exclaimed Kate, making her friends belly laugh again that day.

After a late lunch the women decided to seize the opportunity and do some shopping. It felt good to be in the cool air of the casino and out of the sun for a while. They walked the hallways, eyeing exquisite works of art; window shopped jewelry and occasionally strolled into a store for a closer look.

Outside the entrance of Cartier security officers on Segways stood at attention. They wore bulletproof vests, were obviously packing heat, and were ready for action, as if soldiers preparing for war. Before the women could ask what was going on, a portly Vietnamese woman dressed in a Los Angeles Lakers jersey and shorts, yellow high top sneakers, and extremely large green sunglasses, came barreling down the hallway shouting to a man who stood 100 yards away.

"Usha! Usha! Usha in tha! Usha in tha, go!" she screamed, continuously waving her arms in the air.

The four women frantically looked around, observing the chaos before them. The security officers on Segways continued to patrol the area outside Cartier. They began to radio one another as the crowd grew larger. Curiosity was drawing people closer from every direction.

Ily let the group know that high-end fashion stores at Caesars Palace attracted celebrities on occasion, or so Star magazine wrote.

"What's an Usha?" asked Liz.

"I am pretty sure she is trying to say Usher," Hatti whispered to her friends.

"Oh my God is that the beautiful black man with a fabulous body and sensational smile?" questioned Kate.

"Yes and his signature look is a huge diamond stud earring," Ily added.

Hatti turned to face her friends.

"I don't know about the three of you, but if that is in fact Usher this may be my only shot at a rich, successful, beautiful, black man, and I am not going to pass it up pussy footing around out here with the three of you," Hatti firmly stated.

Ily gave Hatti a hug and told her good luck. Liz was game for going into the store with Hatti. She wanted to see what he was buying. Secretly, Liz hoped Usher would instantly fall in love with her, passionately kiss her in front of the crowd, and then whisk her away. She did not speak a word of her lustful contemplations, but rather hiked up her breasts and lathered on lipstick. Ily and Kate did not want to be left in the shadows of the crowd, so they too, put on their big girl pants and agreed to go in.

"If we separate in the store we have a better chance of finding Usher," said Hatti.

"If he is in fact really in there," spoke Ily.

"Yes, but if we separate then only one of us may get to see him," argued Liz.

After a bit of strategizing the four women locked arm in arm and marched toward the entrance of Cartier. Mission: find Usher, woo him, and hope he finds love at first sight. They approached the entrance with heads held high, eyes wide open, panning the scene before them. They had high hopes of a glimpse at Usher.

Ten steps before they reached the entrance two officers on Segway scooters began pushing the crowd backwards. Four large men in black pin stripe suits emerged out of nowhere. They worked methodically, not a word spoken between them. Once the four body guards were in place Usher, two other men about his age, and a woman, exited Cartier and turned left down the hallway. The body guards pulled in tight around them and the police on Segways led the pack back through the forum shops of Caesar's Palace. As fast as they heard about Usher, he was gone.

"Dammit!" Hatti shouted, stomping her foot. "There goes my chance with a rich, black man!"

Liz reaffirmed her frustration and stated, "Now who is going to wine and dine me?"

Kate was on top of her game and had snapped a few photos of Usher and his entourage.

"Don't be so glum. There are plenty more black men for Hatti, rich men for Liz, and celebrities for the Vietnamese women sporting her gorgeous L.A. Lakers frock," concluded Kate.

They laughed having remembered the scene that began the chaos in the first place.

"I would like to gamble a bit before we head back to Harrah's. Anyone else want to join me?" Hatti asked.

Now that she had a taste of winning, Hatti hit a blackjack table or two whenever she could.

"Count me in. I would say we are on a hot streak with all of the exciting events that have happened," said Liz. "What are the two of you going to do?" Hatti asked Ily and Kate.

Kate wanted to sit and review the pictures she had taken and a stiff drink sounded good too.

"I think I will hit up the casino with the two of you," Kate told them.

Ily had spied a Louis Vuitton store a few doors down and wanted to wander back that way in search of an item for her sister. Her birthday was coming up and an authentic L.V. purchase with a picture of Usher from Kate was the ideal gift.

"My sister is obsessed with Louis Vuitton's line of handbags, wallets, and shoes. I think I will head that way and see if I can find her a birthday gift. I will meet the three of you in the casino after I check out the store. From there we can head back to Harrah's pool for a few hours of fun in the sun before dinner at The Range," Ily suggested to her friends.

Kate, Hatti, and Liz bid adieu to Ily and moseyed down the hallway toward the casino. Ily mingled amongst the crowd of people and snapped a few pictures of the stained glass ceiling and Greek God statues. She made her way down to Louis Vuitton and stood at the entrance snapping photos of the storefront to share with her sister back home. She made sure to capture the prominent lettering and large window displays that demonstrated the prestigious air surrounding the storefront.

Tucking her camera back in her shoulder bag, Ily casually strolled around the store admiring the décor, glitzy items in glass cases, and those rare pieces regally placed upon custom shelving. There was clothing with the L.V. logo, an assorted variety of stilettos, sunglasses, and jewelry; yet nothing seemed fitting for Ily's sister or her first authentic Louis Vuitton purchase. She continued to browse, picking items up, looking them over, peaking at the price tag and inevitably returning it to the shelf.

Ily was on her way to the exit when she noticed a glass case with five wallets embossed with the L.V. logo lying on top. There was a sign that indicated a clearance sale. She picked up one of the two tan colored wallets; the other three were brown. The price tag indicated 75% off. The wallets were being sold for $175, a respective price to pay for Mr. Vuitton's custom craftsmanship. To Ily's right someone had approached her, while she stood at the glass case, examining the features of the tan wallet.

"Excuse me, do you have this wallet in bla…?" Ily began to ask.

Before she could finish her question Ily realized the person standing inches away from her was not a sales clerk, but rather, The Mr. Usher and all his chocolaty goodness.

Ily stood motionless, breathless, and mute for what felt like an eternity. Then she spoke.

"Oh, uh you don't work here, do you?" she asked, feeling stupid.

Usher flashed a brilliant white smile, extended his right hand to touch hers and replied, "No, but you are beautiful."

His words were like silk as they crossed his lips. The blood ran to Ily's face causing her to blush and her heart to race.

"Thank you," was all she could manage.

"Do you live here in Nevada?" Usher asked, gently releasing his hold on Ily's hand.

"No. I live in Wisconsin. I am here for our first annual girls' weekend," answered Ily.

Usher peered around seeing no one within sight. Ily looked down at the wallet in a bit of a haze, unsure of all place and time. She had unknowingly dropped the wallet from her hand.

"My friends decided they had enough shopping and headed to the casino. I decided to check out the Louis Vuitton store in hopes of making my first authentic purchase, along with finding a birthday gift for my sister," Ily told Usher.

She was appalled at herself for rambling on like an idiot.

"What did Usher care?" she thought.

"I see," said Usher, melting Ily with his eyes.

She tried to turn the conversation back toward Usher by asking if he was from the Las Vegas area.

"I have a home near Red Rock," Usher was explaining, when a young woman casually dressed in jeans and t-shirt made her way over and rudely interrupted the conversation.

"Like, how unprofessional. They don't even have my size in stock. Let's go," she whined.

Usher looked back at Ily, took her hand in his once again, and gently kissed the top.

"It was a pleasure meeting you. What did you say your name is?" Usher asked.

"I didn't say," she stated. "My name is Ily."

Usher gave her hand a slight squeeze.

"I am Usher. Do enjoy your stay in Las Vegas, Ily from Wisconsin," he said, looking good enough to lick.

"I know who you are and it was also nice to meet you, Usher from somewhere near Red Rock," she teased, giving him a sultry stare.

They both laughed, he gave her a quick wink, and turned towards the whiny woman he was hanging out with. At that moment, Usher, the casually dressed woman, the other two men and their entourage exited the store.

Usher, a gorgeous, polite, well-dressed man, who smelled oh so scrumptious, had entered her life and exited as fast as he had moments before at Cartier. Ily was left standing in place with a dumb-found look on her face.

The store clerks went about straightening shelves, serving customers, and ringing up purchases. Ily picked up the wallet that had caught her attention before the Usher encounter. She walked in a daze to the register replaying the scene in her head.

"Did you find everything you were looking for today?" the sales clerk asked, as she scanned the wallet and placed it in a bag.

"All that and then some," Ily remarked, secretly alluding to having met Usher.

"I am such an idiot," she thought.

She should have pretended not to know him from any other gorgeous black man with a gigantic diamond earring. She also could have invited him to meet her and her friends for drinks or dinner that evening, but no she just stood there staring at him like some awestruck teen.

"Wait until the girls hear about this," she thought.

In the casino, Ily found her friends circled around a grouping of Wheel of Fortune slot machines. A small crowd had formed to watch the three women play. There was laughing, cheering, and high-fives flying everywhere. Ily saw Liz slap her hand down on the maximum bet button and pull hard on the reel.

Within seconds the Wheel of Fortune icon lit across the screen. Lights flashed, the crowd roared, and Ily ran to her friends' side with a cheerful hello and group hug.

"Oh my God," shrieked Kate, pointing at the machine.

"Hot damn we are on a roll!" exclaimed Liz.

"Come on girlfriend, we cannot do this without you. Get your little ass in here," commanded Hatti.

The crowd that had formed to witness the excitement disbursed with only a few remaining onlookers. Liz, Kate, Hatti, and Ily all placed a gentle, yet confident hand over the button labeled spin.

"On the count of three," instructed Liz.

The others nodded in agreement.

"One....two....three!"

All eyes looked up as the wheel spun round and round. The dinging, pinging sounds of the casino seemed to fade in the distance. The only lights they truly saw were those illuminating the wheel that stood to tell the fate of their takings. The wheel slowed and the four women grasped one another's hands in angst and anticipation. A deep breathe in and...

The wheel clicked once more and stopped on $2000. The silence was deafening. Then the cheers, shouts, tears, and hugs were shared as the celebration began.

"We just won $2000!" yelled Hatti, at the top of her lungs.

The four women jumped up and down continuing to hug and high-five each other, as well as, the crowd that once again began to congregate. After what seemed an eternity of playing Wheel of Fortune, the excitement and laugh lines were embedded deeply around their mouths and eyes. The four women marched to the cage and cashed out at Caesar's Palace.

"I can't believe the luck. It is almost unheard of," Liz confessed.

"That was frickin' insane and felt amazing!" acknowledged Ily.

Liz stopped dead in her tracks to tell her friends she loved them and was having a hell of a time in Vegas. Kate followed by grabbing and pulling them close together. Her smile was pleasant as she extended her arm up and outward for a group picture.

"Everyone say, show me the money!"

The camera flashed, seizing the winning moment for them all to remember in years to come.

CHAPTER 8

Once the fearless foursome had returned to the Harrah's pool there was not an open seat in the house. It appeared everyone had enough of the Nevada heat and thus retreated to the pool.

"Hey, Hollywood! Hollywood! Over here!" called a man's voice.

Liz seductively raised her arm to waive at the men they had met from the cabana earlier that morning.

"What?" she asked, smiling at her friends.

"Hollywood?" inquired Hatti.

"Yeah, that's what I told them my name is," Liz said, grinning ear to ear.

"Nice work Hollywood," said Ily, nudging her with an elbow, smiling.

Liz led the pack around the pool to the cabana and greeted each man with a welcoming hug and kiss leaving behind a ruby red lipstick mark.

"She sure is living up to her name, isn't she?" Hatti whispered to Kate, and they both snickered.

The four women set their belongings on the wicker table beneath the cabana. Introductions were conducted by Liz of all four women. Sparky, who had waved them over, introduced his group of guy friends. Sparky filled the ladies in on what they had missed at the pool while they had gone to eat.

"Not a damn thing. We were hoping the four of you would be back so we had some eye candy again. You sure know how to work a crowd," Sparky notated.

He told them they were waiting for their friend Dan to arrive. His flight was due to land around three o'clock, so they expected him in the next hour or so. The cocktail waitress appeared outside the cabana and took drink orders from the entire group.

She took one look at Hatti and said, "I know what you want."

"The bartender," Hatti said, bluntly.

The men and women laughed at her wit.

"One delicious David drink made with banana daiquiri, completely rum free," the cocktail waitress confirmed.

The women laughed and were impressed by the young lady's memory and humor.

"You've got it, girlfriend," Hatti said, with a wink.

The women removed their clothing down to brightly colored bikinis and climbed into the pool.

"God bless America," said one of the men, as they, too, jumped in and joined the four women in the sparkling water.

Sparky and Liz were the last two to enter the pool. They had remained in the cabana bantering back and forth with each other about whether or not Sparky could jump over Liz's head while standing in the pool.

"Doubtful," said Liz, in a cocky, I-dare-you-to voice. "I am 5'9" head to toe and half of me is sticking out of the water. There is no way you would make it," she challenged.

Sparky's friends were already placing side bets and Kate, Hatti, and Ily slowly backed away from them.

"He'll never make it," said Kate, panicked.

"He won't even come close," Ily agreed.

Hatti peeked between split fingers as Liz climbed into the pool and gave a shout out drawing the focus of pool-goers her way.

"Attention, attention everyone!" Liz bellowed. "Watch as the amazing Sparky jumps over my head into the pool."

All heads turned to the cabana as Sparky came barreling out like a Green Bay Packer linebacker defending the end zone. When he hit the edge of the pool Sparky leapt into the air, spread eagle, hands flailing about wildly. Liz let out a deafening scream, shut her eyes, and stood as still as a statue. Sparky flew straight at her. His graceful hurtle nearly cleared the top of her head with the exception of his balls smashing into her forehead.

The crowd gasped in horror as Liz flew backwards and sank beneath the water. Hatti, Kate, and Ily were left standing there terrified, only a few feet away from the scene. Was her neck snapped? Would Sparky's balls be stuck to her forehead when she emerged?

Seconds felt like an eternity before the first sign of Sparky emerging from the water occurred. He was holding his nut sack and groaning miserably. Liz popped up out of the water in front of him looking like a drowned cat. Her hair was matted to her face and mascara ran wildly down her cheeks. She raised her right arm with un-spilled drink in hand.

The crowd cheered uncontrollably now that everyone was alright. Liz bent down, sucked up a mouth full of pool water and spewed it from her lips like the fountains outside Bellagio. The crowd's cheers turned to noises of disgust knowing that half the people in the pool hadn't gotten out of the water all day to use the restroom.

Sparky's friends moved in for high-fives, knuckles, and ass slaps. Liz and her friends came together for a group hug. Kate gave them the official replay, laughing and gasping between details. After 20 minutes of reliving the moment Sparky balled Liz in the forehead, play by play, and some parts in slow motion; the conversation turned as the newest member of the men's group arrived.

"Dan's here!" Sparky shouted, pointing to the opposite side of the pool.

Dan had a look of shock about him as he walked towards the cabana. He had no clue who the women were with his friends, but his widening smile indicated that he did not seem to mind. Dan wore a short sleeved, button down shirt, that was light blue and white checked, with jeans and Dockers sandals. He looked over-dressed for the weather in Vegas. Slung over his shoulder was a navy blue duffle bag containing his clothing and necessities for the week. Dan had more light brown hair on his face than on his head. He resembled the actor who played Al Borland on the television sitcom, Home Improvement.

"Dan! Oh Dan, you made it," Liz cried out.

Completely out of control, Liz bounded across the concrete patio and sprang into Dan's arms, wrapping her legs around his waist. She squeezed tightly and christened him with one of her red lipstick kisses. It was a good thing Dan stood 6'2", had broad shoulders, and enough muscle to support his weight and hers too. Dan looked shocked.

"Who is this?" he asked, holding Liz up around his waist.

"Hollywood," yelled just about everyone in the pool.

"Well, nice to meet you Hollywood!" remarked Dan.

"The pleasure is all mine," Liz said, excitedly.

She slid down the front of Dan like a human fire-pole leaving two water marks where her wet breasts penetrated his shirt.

Kate, Hatti, Liz, Ily, Sparky, Dan, and the other patrons at the pool soaked up the sun and rum for the remainder of the afternoon. Around 6:00 p.m., the crowd began to thin. Sparky and his crew had abandoned the cabana, acknowledging they would be back tomorrow to set up camp if the four women cared to join them again. They wished each other big winnings and a safe and fun evening. A life guard circled the poolside announcing closing time and demanding people exit the water.

"Let's just hang out for a bit yet. There are enough people that have to pull their things together and leave before we have to get out," said Liz.

They were having such a remarkable time. Not one of them was ready for this day to end.

"It sure is relaxing out here," commented Hatti, resting her head on the edge of the pool.

"It sure is now that all of the male piranhas have left," teased Kate, giving Ily a nudge.

The four women floated easily in the pool reminiscing the day's events. The pool boy circled around for a second time making his way over to them. He was no more than 20 years old, tall, athletic, and just a baby in their eyes. His skin was tanned, his hair a mess from a long hot day manning his post on the life guard station. He was a pleasant young man, polite, and patient with guests.

"Excuse me ladies. I have to ask you to leave the pool now," he instructed, in a calm, rational voice.

The four women continued to float in the water, smiling ear to ear under the spell of alcohol and adrenaline.

"Already?" questioned Liz, playing dumb.

"Yes," he answered with a sigh, anticipating a struggle from these four women.

They were now the only ones remaining at the pool.

"Tell you what, why don't you take off your pants, get in the pool, and we'll talk about it," Ily suggested.

The pool boy's dark eyes grew wide and a look of surprise came over his face. He bent down next to the water and motioned for Ily to come closer. He was young and had dealt with women like her before. He was just as ready to play as they were.

"Are you always this sassy?" he asked, looking her straight in the eye.

"Do you want me to be?" inquired Ily, now playing along with his game.

He laughed in retort at her wit and charm. Kate, Hatti and Liz moved in closer to Ily.

"Please ladies, just get out of the pool," he begged.

"Ok we will," Ily agreed, "If you bring us each a dry towel and wrap us up as we get out of the water."

"Respect your elders and do as you're told," taunted Hatti.

The four women watched in amazement as he strutted towards the towel table. He was so young and so vulnerable. It almost seemed sinful to mess with him.

"Too bad we are so old," said Kate, eyeing the young pool boy.

"Speak for yourself," cautioned Hatti, making a cougar noise.

He returned with four dry, fluffy, white towels and set them next to the ladder. He looked at the four women and spoke only one word, "Out!"

He smiled a toothy grin, so as not to appear too hostile.

"Okay, okay," the four women said, as they waved their imaginary white flags to show they surrendered and intended to oblige his wishes and exit the pool.

Ily moved to the ladder, and when she reached the top the pool boy wrapped her tightly in a towel and spanked her.

"Seriously?" she asked. "Did you just spank me?"

They were all laughing and raving over the balls this young kid was now demonstrating.

"Two can play this game," he said, and winked.

Liz swam to the ladder next and pulled herself up out of the water. Again he grabbed a towel and draped it around her body. In evidence of his newly found confidence with the women he pulled Liz close to him and dipped her backwards, as if they had just wrapped up a ballroom dance. Liz, in return, pulled his head close to hers and kissed his forehead, leaving her lip prints on yet another male in the Nevada desert.

"Well done," he said, releasing her from his grip.

Hatti had concocted a plan for how she would greet this spunky pool boy when it was her turn to exit the water. She grabbed hold of the railing, pulled herself out of the water and with a fling of her damp hair exclaimed, "Here comes your wet dream, baby!"

A wave of laughter washed over all of them. The pool boy had no response. He was shocked by the brazenness of these four women.

"Who are they," he wondered.

The young, sun-kissed pool boy bent down, picked up the fourth towel and turned to face Kate.

"Well, show me what you got, girl!" he said.

Kate swam to the ladder, grabbed hold, pulled herself out of the water, and portraying a very brutish woman said, "And here comes your worst nightmare!"

Laughter and shrills of delight emanated all around.

"You are a genius!" Ily proclaimed.

The pool boy carried out his end of the deal and swaddled Kate in her towel, slapped her ass, dipped her backward, and kissed her forehead.

"Ba da boom, ba da bang!" he concluded, throwing her to the side.

All four women were still laughing heartily as they left the pool and headed for their hotel room. Liz and Hatti had to cross their legs so as not to wet their pants. The pool boy went home that night having no clue who they were, but knew he would not soon forget, the last four women at the Harrah's pool that evening.

CHAPTER 9

Kate slipped her card into the lock. As they entered the room they noticed a lot had changed since that morning. The lights came on with a flick of the switch, the mini bar hummed quietly in the corner, the bathtub was empty, the room temperature was comfortable enough not to wear a snow suit, and the countertop that had crashed beneath the weight of Liz's suitcase was mounted on the wall again.

"What the hell happened in here?" questioned Kate, not believing anyone could undo the disaster they had left behind earlier that morning.

"Who cleaned up our swamp, Fiona," Ily teased, stepping on dry carpet, which hours before had felt like a bog.

Hatti walked over to the mini bar, opened the door, and said, "Somebody's been in our room and fixed the mini bar!"

Kate from the other side of the room carried on the fairy tale announcing, "And somebody took the booze from the bathtub!"

Liz finished it off by stating, "And somebody picked up my shit for me, too!"

Ily turned to her friends and pretended to look horrified.

"Who would ever think to ruin the fun we spent hours in this room creating?" she asked.

Liz, looking more like Tammy Baker with her mascara strewn about her face, pretended to be tearing up over the clean, pulled together room.

"They're all a bunch of fuckers!" she yelled, and fell on the bed giggling.

Hatti whipped open the front of the cherry wood armoire and cranked up the volume on the radio when Bon Jovi's, "Shot Through the Heart," came on. She also noticed a white box with a red ribbon tied around it. On top was a note with nothing written on the envelope.

"Hey guys, check this out. Someone left us a gift," Hatti called out.

She peeled open the envelope and pulled out a simple piece of stationery with the Harrah's logo. Hatti read out loud for her friends.

"Ladies, it was wonderful spending time with you all at Toby Keith's Bar. If you are reading this note you have found your room put back in order. Enjoy The Range Steakhouse this evening. I wish I could have made it, too. In the morning, pack your bags, and dial extension 5527. Let the woman who answers the phone know you are ready for the limousine to take you to the Paris Casino and Hotel. Your room has been reserved under Ily's name. I hope you enjoyed the day at the pool. I know I enjoyed watching you from the fitness center! It was a warm Las Vegas day and I am anticipating tomorrow night to be even hotter. Ily, Kate mentioned it is your birthday. Happy Birthday! Chef Tim made this especially for you. Enjoy. I am looking forward to La Burger Brassiere, tomorrow evening, 9:15 p.m., sharp! See you lovely ladies then. Respectfully, Nolan."

The four women gaped at one another in amazement. Kate was the first to comment.

"Let me get this straight. An extremely wealthy, powerful, supposedly single man, buys our drinks all evening, sends a restoration team to repair our room because Ily declines his offer to switch rooms, he remembers our names during a special visit poolside, then has a beautiful cake prepared for Ily, and is now paying for our room at Paris tomorrow night?" questioned Kate.

They all looked at one another bewildered.

"He's a nice guy," Liz stated, innocently.

"Oh come on," Ily scolded, narrowing her eyes at the naiveté of her friend.

"I bet he is expecting one of us to take one for the team," Hatti admitted.

They all looked at Ily.

"Oh no!" she exclaimed. "I love you bitches, but I am not sleeping with some disease infested Las Vegas Lone Ranger, so forget it. And besides, by the looks of Kate's pictures from last night he already made it with Liz!"

Liz's face turned to a look of disgust and her voice had a hint of jealousy.

"The only reason he sat by me was to ask questions about you, Ily. Majority of the time he came across so self-consumed I didn't care to entertain his thoughts. I love you Ily and he just doesn't seem the right fit for you. I doubt he has time for a relationship with any woman. I made sure he knew you were not on the market at this time," remarked Liz.

Ily thanked her friend for having her best interests at heart.

"Well, in that case, his best bet is me!" Hatti volunteered. "I love 'em and leave 'em," she explained.

"I am not sure how appealing Nolan's goods are but this cake looks pretty orgasmic," Kate chimed in.

Ily pulled the cake out of the box while her friends sang happy birthday to her. Ily's thoughts were still mixed with booze and far from focused. Without hesitation she took the beautiful cake and smashed it into Kate's face.

"You are such a bitch," shouted Kate, from behind three inches of frosting.

Kate reached into the box, scooped up a handful of cake and aimed for Ily. As her arm came across her body, Ily ducked and the cake flew out of Kate's hand right into Hatti's face. Hatti dove for the box, palmed a clump of the cake, turned around, and smeared it across Liz's chest.

"Cake fight!" yelled Ily, grabbing another handful and chasing Kate out of the room.

Liz ran behind seeking revenge. Sporting bikinis and covered in sugary goodness, the women continued the cake fight out into the hallway. Hatti flung the door wide open, making her way out after her friends. Instantly aware of what was about to happen, all four women turned back toward the hotel room, just as the door slammed shut. Their arms reached through the air and jaws dropped to the floor.

"No!" they yelled, in unison.

Frozen in the moment and realizing no one thought to grab a key, they began to panic.

"Security! Security!" Ily yelled, in her best Bon Qui Qui voice.

They stood drenched in cake and frosting, blaming Hatti, because she was the last one out of the room. Hatti, being the most sensible of the intoxicated women, was adamantly trying to defend her position.

"Ily, this is entirely your fault," she stated, firmly. "You ruined a beautiful cake from Nolan, there is frosting all over the room, and now we have to face security for what you have done."

Ily only laughed at Hatti's maturity and state of panic.

"Shut the hell up, Hatti. You know we'll get out of this," Ily assured her.

Ily enjoyed confrontations with Hatti and respected their opposite demeanor. Ily wiped a handful of cake and frosting mixture from the white box she still held in her hand. As she lunged toward Hatti, she managed to catch her neck and cheek with the sugary concoction once again. Hatti had learned over their years of friendship that with Ily in a complete manic mood the best thing to do is release your inhibitions and join her craziness.

"All right you nutball," Hatti relinquished, giving Ily a hug. "Let's see how you get us out of this one."

Liz was coming down from the rush and explained that she was not going to jail in the Nevada prison for any of them.

Kate disagreed with her, adding, "To hell with it. I will gladly call home from the clink. They're all a bunch of fuckers anyway."

Just then security rounded the corner and strolled down the hallway towards their room. He was an extremely tall, slender, serious looking individual. He definitely made the uniform look good. In his right hand he held a radio and in the left, a billy club. He looked serious as he walked slowly down the corridor toward them.

The security guard's look of concern made the women's anxiety run wild. The four women stood covered in cake, dripping with frosting in their bathing suits, wearing the look of a new puppy who had just chewed the sofa to pieces.

"What have we here?" he questioned, struggling to hold back a smile.

There was a brief moment of silence and the stories began to pour out.

"Well, you see officer, there were these kids next door and they really like cake...." Ily began.

"Yeah, they pushed us over when we came back from the pool," Liz added.

Kate was trying to keep a straight face while she summed it up stating in a distressed tone, "Those boys just pushed us down, stole our cake, and when we tried to get it back they threw it at us! Can you believe that?"

The officer stood towering above them, cocked his eyebrow and asked, "These boys, did you get a good look at them? How old are they?"

He was messing with the women now, amused by their playful innocence.

"Ten," Hatti stated, in more of a question than answer.

All heads turned her way.

"Ten?" The officer repeated.

They couldn't help but snicker. It was all just too much, and far beyond reality.

As the officer verbally confirmed the details of their story, the four women nodded their heads in agreement. They were like four naughty children awaiting their punishment.

Then he spoke, "Let me get this straight; you were jumped while entering your hotel room, had a cake stolen from your property, were the victims of assault as they pushed you aside to flee the scene of the crime, and the only description you have of the alleged birthday cake thieves is that they were 10 year olds?"

"And boys," Ily added, confidently, implying a missed and important detail.

Her friends all nodded in agreement.

"What we have here is a random act of assault and battery, breaking and entering, theft, and fleeing the scene of a crime. How would you like me to proceed with capture of the perpetrators and charges thereafter?" questioned the officer.

The four women looked back and forth astonished it had come to this. They quickly wrapped their arms around one another's shoulders, as if in a football huddle, to discuss the officer's words and their next play.

"Oh my God, we are screwed!" Hatti hissed.

"Shhhh, don't panic. Just let me handle this. You three look sexy and keep your mouths shut," Ily ordered.

They broke from the huddle and turned to face the extremely tall officer.

"Your honor, officer, sir, we realize that we don't have much of a description to aid in the efforts of an arrest. So, we were thinking, how about letting us back into our room and we will just forget all about this little incident?" Ily casually suggested.

Ily gave a wink to her friends and crossed her fingers behind her back.

The officer looked at Ily and then the three women standing seductively behind her. They were allowing her to take the initial heat emanating off his face. He checked his watch and with a sigh he used his large hand to wipe his face from the brow down to his chin.

"Whose name is the room under," he asked.

Ily meekly raised her hand. Towering over her he looked her up and down.

The officer cleared his throat and spoke, "I am going to need to see some identification. However, based on what you are and are not wearing, I am going to guess it is in there."

He pointed to the hotel room door.

Ily never felt so naked standing before a complete stranger in her life. She recoiled hoping he was not aware of her sheer embarrassment.

Ily raised her big green eyes to his, batted them once or twice, and said, "Yes."

That was all she could manage at the moment.

The awkward silence was broken by a woman's voice over the radio he had been holding. The dispatcher was asking if Officer Pryor needed back up.

"What do you think of Officer Pryor," Liz whispered to her friends.

Hatti wondered if Officer Pryor's package in his pants followed suit with his height and hand size. Ily caught her friend gaping at the bulge beneath his navy slacks and smacked Hatti across the head.

"Stop undressing him with your eyes! We are in enough trouble," Ily scolded.

Officer Pryor confirmed the name on the room with the woman on the other end of the radio, pulled out a master room key, and unlocked the door. Still covered in cake and frosting, Liz, Kate, and Hatti ran for the powder room, while Ily rummaged through her purse for two forms of identification. Officer Pryor remained in the entry way scanning the room in surveillance. Ily presented her driver's license and credit card, wiped a hunk of frosting from her eyebrow, and smiled brightly.

"See it's me! Now, I have a favor to ask you, Officer Pryor. Could we get a picture with you?" Ily inquired, boldly.

Shouts came from the bathroom to shut up, knock it off, don't be stupid, just let him get out of here and so on, and yet Ily stood proud of the moment and the fact that they had escaped trouble once again. Officer Pryor stood in the entrance silent for a moment, then smiled, and called for the other three women to come out of the bathroom.

Kate, Hatti and Liz barged from behind the door with excitement. The four women and Officer Pryor smiled wide for the camera capturing the picture which would remind them for years to come of the mischievous cake fight at Harrah's hotel.

CHAPTER 10

Dinner that evening was spectacular. The Range Steakhouse offered low lighting, a glitter and glitz atmosphere, and spectacular treatment. The four women were dressed for an elegant evening out, in Las Vegas.

Ily wore a simple, spaghetti strap, black dress, and sexy silver heels. Her auburn hair hung long and straight down her back allowing the colors to play in the light. Her makeup was soft and her green eyes popped against her sun-kissed skin. Ily made her own jewelry out of Swarzski crystals, which glistened beneath the chandelier as she stepped off the elevator.

Liz looked simply amazing too. Her tanned legs stretched long and lean beneath a single strap red dress that hung just a bit longer in the back than the front. Her breasts were the largest of the four women and she often teased the others about her blessing and their lack thereof. This evening she chose to draw attention to her bust with an oversized necklace and dangling pendant that lay nestled amongst her cleavage. She wore simple black heels and a silver bracelet, so as not to draw attention away from her bosom.

Kate chose a white dress with large gold earrings, gold bangle bracelets, and strappy gold heels. Her bleach-blonde hair and pixie cut made her look as though she belonged showcased at Caesar's Palace. She looked radiant and much younger than her years.

Hatti was sexy and sophisticated, in a black halter top, bedazzled in silver glitter swirls, and flowing wide leg black pants. She was the shortest of the four women but her silver stilettos made her appear much taller this evening. Her natural strawberry blonde hair was pulled back, accentuating her cheekbones and full lips.

Men gawked and women eyeballed each of the four women as they entered the dining room and took their seats at table number eight. Whispers all around were heard as people tried to determine who these women were.

The waiter approached, placing linen napkins across their laps, and distributing menus. They ordered wine and shrimp cocktail for the table. A trio of men strummed instruments on a small stage, setting the mood for a light and easy evening. The wine flowed and the laughs continued between friends.

The meal was exquisitely composed of a vegetable medley, steak, soup and salad.

"What a fine feast!" exclaimed Liz.

Hours later the four women sat back enjoying the soft music and a cup of coffee. They were full of fine food and wine, feeling happy and sated.

"This vacation was a must for me and I am thankful to relish in each moment of it with the three of you," said Kate, a bit teary eyed.

"Oh stop your crying. You will make a mess of your perfect face," Ily told her, leaning over and wiping a tear from her cheek.

The waiter approached with the bill and a little slice of chocolate and strawberry heaven for each of them.

Hatti looked curiously at the waiter and stated, "I don't mean to be rude, as this looks lovely, but we didn't order dessert."

The waiter smiled and simply stated, "You women have been a pleasure to have in our company this evening. You have drawn the curiosity of the men seated at table 20. They are here for the convention. I hope dessert is something you can manage, as it is our most delectable item on the menu."

He told them to enjoy and he would return to collect their dues momentarily. Liz, Hatti, Ily, and Kate glanced over at table 20 where at least a dozen gorgeous, well-dressed men, sat enjoying Chivas.

"Pinch me," ordered Liz.

"I know, girlfriend, are you thinking what I am thinking?" questioned Hatti.

Kate chimed in at that moment stating, "This is way too good to be true. Men don't dress like that, look like that, or act like this, unless they are horny, married on the prowl for sex, or gay."

They waved toward table 20, mouthing the words, *"thank you,"* and enjoyed their complimentary dessert. The waiter returned to collect the bill and payment for dinner after refilling their coffee cups.

"I assume all was well for you ladies?" questioned the waiter.

"Absolutely delightful," replied Ily, speaking for the group.

Moments passed when the waiter returned to the table with a strange expression on his face. He stood at the head of the table for a moment before speaking.

"Ladies, would you happen to have another form of payment than cash?" he questioned them.

Liz looked at Hatti, Hatti looked at Ily, and Ily turned to Kate.

"What do you mean other than cash? You don't accept cash here?" questioned Kate.

"Madame, my superior believes some of the 20 dollar bills may be counterfeit and has requested an alternative form of payment. My sincere apologies, ladies," the waiter grimaced.

At that instant you could have heard a pin drop. Shock overtook the women and they sat motionless at the thought of having been in the possession of counterfeit money in Vegas.

"Are you fucking kidding me?" Ily finally spoke.

"No ma'am. Do you have another way to pay for the bill?"

Not sure what to do in the moment, Ily pulled out her credit card and handed it to the waiter. He thanked them and indicated he would return. As the shock wore off they began to laugh a nervous laugh.

"I don't believe it!" exclaimed Kate, under her breath.

"I want to see what the bills look like," said Hatti.

Liz was replaying in her mind the places they had been were money was exchanged. They could have acquired the counterfeit money anywhere. The waiter returned with Ily's credit card and thanked them for a wonderful evening and understanding. He returned the cash to the women and before he could walk away they were holding the bills high in the air thoroughly examining them for fraudulent markings.

"I don't know about you, but I think the bills look legit," said Hatti.

They stood from the table, waved good-bye to their admirers at table 20, made their way back to the elevator, and down to the casino.

"Do you ladies realize we just tried to pay for almost $600 worth of food with potential counterfeit money?" proclaimed Ily.

They were still experiencing disbelief over the situation. Laughing out loud, Kate wondered what the waiter thought having served four women dressed to the nine's, endless glasses of wine, and an expensive meal. The same four women who then decline dessert, until they are aware that it is free, and proceed to pay the bill with counterfeit money!

"I totally knew something was strange about those bills," said Liz.

"Oh, the hell if you did Liz," exclaimed Ily.

"You are all lucky I thought to carry my credit card with me. You each owe me and you owe me big time. And, by the way, you are all a bunch of fuckers!" Ily stated, matter-of-factly.

The other three women thanked Ily for being the smartest, best in the bunch, as they walked arm in arm back to their hotel room.

CHAPTER 11

"Rise and shine, it is Paris time!" Hatti shouted, waking her friends from a remarkable night's sleep.

Typically in Las Vegas, when the lights go down, life picks up, but for these four women it had been a long couple of days. The rest and relaxation the evening before was welcomed. Their belongings were packed and ready for the move to Paris. Ily was still unsure as to the reason the room was compliments of Nolan.

As instructed, Ily called the number on the card he had given her, and within minutes a bellhop was at their door to transport luggage. Down the elevator, bright eyed and bushy tailed, the four women hit up Starbucks and left Harrah's feeling ready to take on the town once again.

The limousine driver stood dutifully at attention outside the sleek, jet black car. He had been given specific instructions to take good care of Hatti, Kate, Liz, and Ily. He had a nice smile, was about 5'6" tall, and his protruding belly announced his fondness for beer.

The initial arrival at Paris was breathtaking. People, people, and more people entered taxis, exited limos, and wandered in and out of the double, gold doors leading into the casino. To the right were long lines of folks checking in for the night, the weekend, or the week. Hatti was so excited she ran to the red ropes and stood in line with a meaningful presence, while the other three women made their way over to her side.

Their room was absolutely stunning. The four women stood at the window, peering out over the pool, eyeing the Eiffel tower replica, and watching in amazement as the Bellagio water show took their breath away. They settled their belongings in the green and purple colored room.

The sleeping area held two double beds, a dresser, and huge flat screen television. The sitting room was comprised of a cherry wood desk, long green sofa, deep-set, purple chairs, and gold trimmed tables. The dining area was fitted with a round table for four, a wet bar, and paintings of the French countryside. Around the corner they found his and her restrooms each with an oversize whirlpool tub and shower. Most of all, Liz liked the bidet.

All four women jumped when the telephone on the desk between the two double beds began to ring. Kate answered and the automated female voice on the other end began to speak. She was seeking to ensure the room was satisfactory and went on whispering in a French accent about the amenities offered at Paris Casino. Liz found a platter in the refrigerator heaping with various fruits, berries, and assorted cheeses. The four women dined on the spread, drank mimosas and dressed for an afternoon at the Paris pool.

Just before they left the room the table top telephone rang again.

"Hello," answered Liz. "Hi Nolan! Yes we made it and the room is exquisite….sure, we will be there at 9:15 p.m. sharp."

Liz hung up the phone and turned toward her friends.

"Can you believe this? That was Nolan and he said that if we are at La Burger Brassiere before he arrives to let them know that we are his guests and food and drinks are on the house," shrieked Liz.

"Did you tell him we are not thinking about that, because we have a whole day ahead of us at the pool?" retorted Hatti.

She was already in her bathing suit with an obnoxiously large beach bag slung over her shoulder. She was not going to miss a thing now that she had gotten the opportunity to see, stay and play at Paris.

The other three women took their time dressing in bathing suits, organizing themselves in the room and preparing for a day at the pool.

"I don't think I could laugh any harder today than I did yesterday," Hatti commented, hiking her shoulder bag back over her arm, as they exited the hotel room and made their way to the elevator.

When the door opened they met a group of men who were also headed to the pool. They appeared to be having fun and were quite liquored up. Ily pretended to be from Great Britain and spoke with a British accent to the men.

"Cheerio!" she said joyfully. "We're British. Where are you bloody bastards from?"

Her friend's burst out laughing at Ily's pathetic British accent. The men looked at her with odd expressions, and then joined the laughter turning to face one of the men standing to the back of the elevator.

"Good day. My name is Scott, from Scotland," he stated.

His British accent was legit. Liz thought about changing her tune, but decided to challenge him instead.

"Oh, really?" questioned Liz, giving her best British accent. "Show me your passport then, lad."

Scott from Scotland did not miss a beat as he reached around his backside, and withdrew his passport from his pocket.

"There, you see. I am a true Brit. Now, do tell us where you beautiful, lying women are really from."

"Fuckwitage," mumbled Ily, under her breath.

Kate spoke up and said, "We're from Wisconsin."

The group of men laughed harder hearing Kate's thick accent, which made her blush. They continued to chat casually as the whole group headed outdoors to the pool. They parted ways on the patio to find the remaining few available lounge chairs. The pool at Paris was much nicer than the Olympic size rectangle at Harrah's, and the desert heat warranted water of any kind that morning. The first thing the women noticed was the enormous Eiffel tower protruding from the far right corner of the sun deck. It seemed to touch the tips of the clouds, glowing golden in the sunlight.

"Absolutely amazing," gasped Kate, taking a picture of the erect structure.

Climbing vines, boasting colored flowers, wrapped themselves around numerous arches encircling a prestine, aqua blue swimming pool. The vegetation was immaculate, the smell of fresh flowers was ever present, and the music played just loud enough to hear over the crowd.

Once they found a section of the patio, with four available lounge chairs and a small round white table, the four women hunkered down, removed their cover ups, and strutted to the pool's edge.

"This is more beautiful than I imagined," Hatti commented, desperately seeking to take it all in.

Ily was amazed at the scene around her and felt quite comfortable there. She wished her home had some of the beauty and grace of French style. Flowers like this just do not sustain well in Wisconsin.

Kate and Liz leaned against the edge of the pool with their arms spanned out to hold their heads above water. The temperature was heating up and the sun was making an appearance over the top of the Cosmopolitan resort. It was going to be another beautiful Las Vegas day.

A round of rum runners arrived and of course, a banana daiquiri for Hatti, since she was still bowled over about losing the rum bet to Ily. She wanted to make good on the $100. she owed Ily, so Hatti bought the first round of drinks for everyone.

They laughed and talked amongst themselves for a while and were surprised when the group of men from the elevator swam over.

Scott from Scotland was the first to speak as the others stared, bearing smirks on their faces.

"Well, fancy meeting you here, my good lad," Ily teased.

"Indeed," replied Scott, from Scotland.

Introductions took place and before long Ily, Hatti, Liz and Kate were best of friends with another group of strangers. It is amazing how alcohol, sun, and a crazy place like Vegas can bring folks from all over the world together for one afternoon.

The four women had learned that their friends arrived earlier that morning and were participating in or attending a friend's wedding that evening. The groom sat on the edge of the pool near Kate and drank conservatively, while his cronies drank buckets of Coors light for hours on end.

Bobby, the usher in the wedding, asked if the four women had ever seen Shamu. Those that had been to Sea World said they had and asked why. Bobby proceeded to pull down his swim trunks, complete a full circle somersault in the pool, bare his white ass and fart at just the right time to create the image of a whale blowhole. Everyone gasped in horror at the sight of Bobby's enormous white ass, the view of his black hole, and the disgusting wisps of air and water mixed spraying from his rear for the grand finale.

The female lifeguard working that particular end of the pool panicked at the production and blew her whistle at him consecutively until Bobby pulled his pants back up. It was an image no one would soon forget. He was forever after, referred to as Bobby, the Baby Beluga!

Ily, Hatti, Liz, and Kate decided to make their way to the hot tubs for a change of pace. The rum runners where setting in and sobriety was no longer an option for the afternoon.

CHAPTER 12

The four women strolled across the patio, down the gray and peach paved walkway beneath arches of lush greens, trimmed at the base with an assortment of red, purple, and white hibiscus and bougusvillianer. The to the two oversize Jacuzzis called out to them. The one to the right was unoccupied, and five men in their early forties occupied the other.

"Eenie, meenie, minie moe," Ily called out, flipping her finger back and forth from each Jacuzzi making sure it landed on the left.

The men in the Jacuzzi smiled wide knowing the four women would be gracing them with their bikini bodies.

"Hello, gents," Ily said, in her lousy British accent.

"Where are you ladies from?" questioned the men, with raised eyebrows.

"We're from Brit…oh forget it. We're from good old Wisconsin," Kate contributed.

The men laughed hardily at Kate's Wisconsin accent. This was quickly becoming a trend. Most people enjoyed her native accent more than the pretending. Names were exchanged and handshakes took place. The men said they were from New York. They were in Vegas for work and today, play. Paris sponsored an event for their company the night before and today they were free to relax.

Relax they did. Jokes were told, stories from the past days were swapped, and the women's newfound friends from New

York were in disbelief of the phenomenal stories Hatti, Liz, Kate, and Ily told them.

Another round of rum runners went down like water and soon the conversations turned perverted. Ily tried to convince the New Yorkers that her small breasts were implants and that she didn't want to go, too big, like everyone else.

"Besides," she said, "I only saved enough money to purchase one size C, so they split it!"

Everyone laughed as she demonstrated her version of the breast stroke and pretended as though her breasts were keeping her afloat. Ily exited the hot tub, stood behind the bald headed man, and squeezed her breasts together. The water that had soaked up in her bikini top's padding was released with a rush over his head. He was caught off guard at first, but then tipped his head back and drank the water feverously. Every man at the pool wished to the heaven's Ily would stand above him and squeeze water from her breasts.

Jimmy, from New York, said he recently had a penis implant and that was why his dick was floating straight up at the moment too. His friends thought this was hilarious.

Liz asked the men if they knew what Wisconsin hardwood floors looked like. They cocked their heads to the side waiting to see what would become of her comment. Even though they were from New York they found this group of women to be quite fascinating, ballsy and fun.

"Hardwood floors," said Liz. "You know, smooth as a baby's ass below."

The men shook their heads no in answer to her question. Liz pulled the bottom of her bathing suit to the side for the world to see hardwood floors.

"Oh my God!" gasped one of the men.

"No way she just did that!" said another.

Ily, Kate, and Hatti laughed at the surprise and shock from the men when they learned that a clean shave was no longer recognized as a Brazilian wax, but rather known as, sporting hardwood floors. The laughter continued and the women never ceased to amaze anyone with their stories. Ily entered into a wrestling match with the youngest of the group of men. She wrapped her scrawny arms around his neck and took down the 200 pound guy. Under the water they went. When they emerged, Ily had her thighs wrapped around his neck in a choke hold. He spun around and slammed them both under the water again. Bets were being placed that eventually Ily would tire him out and win the match.

Ily and the man from New York continued to toss and turn in the water pounding the shit out of each other through alcohol induced fun. She called him a pussy, and he laughed, saying when he won he was going to eat pussy, not be one.

In the last round, Mr. New York put Ily in a Half Nelson hold. She thrust her body backwards trying to knock him over into the water, but instead clocked him in the face with the backside of her head. He released his hold, clutched his hands over his nose, as the blood began to run down his face.

"Shit," he laughed, all pissed up and feeling no pain.

His friend threw a towel at him as he exited the water.

Liz made the sound of a bell ringing and raised Ily's hand high in the air. Ily then made her way over to her opponent and gave him a big hug and kiss on the cheek, letting him know she hoped she didn't hurt him too badly.

"Nah, no worries, beautiful. I've never had my ass kicked by a woman before. It was fun, you know," he replied, smiling with blood stained teeth.

His friends loved this. Money was exchanged between those who bet on Ily winning the match and those who lost teased and tormented the New Yorker for having lost to a lady. The men in the Jacuzzi that day, with these four women, duly noted this was going to be the story they took home to their friends.

Back at their lounge chairs, near the pool, Hatti fell asleep in the sun, while the other three women floated on rafts in the crystal clear water. The wedding party from the elevator, including Scott, from Scotland, and Bobby, (Shamu's brother), swam over to socialize again. Liz talked about Ily whooping ass in the hot tub and Kate acknowledged the fact that he was lucky it was Ily and not Liz who decided to wrestle him for money.

Bobby chimed in stating, "No joke girl, your arms are huge. What do you do for a living?"

"I'm a bounty hunter," Liz replied casually.

"Really?" questioned Bobby, looking to Ily and Kate for confirmation.

"Of course she's a bounty hunter. Look at her, for God's sake. She'd turn you inside out," said Kate.

"We want to hear you say Saturday or casserole," joked one of the men, to Kate.

She obliged, pronounced both words, and even hammed it up a bit by elongating the vowels like any good Wisconsinite. Then Ily and Liz chimed in playing with the group a bit.

"Yah, we eat tuna noodle casserole on Saturdays and green bean casserole on Sunday," said Ily.

The accent was killing them. Everyone they met on their vacation said there is something that tickles your toes and makes you smile, when a Wisconsin woman talks.

At a moment's notice the music changed from something sung in French to a song they recognized. The jock jams theme song boomed from the speakers surrounding the sun deck. A disk jockey piped up on the microphone inviting people to participate in the Paris pool dance-off. He stated the competition would begin in 20 minutes.

"Let's check this out. I bet it'll be fun. Enjoy your *Saturday*," said Kate, exiting the pool to rejoin Hatti, who was still passed out poolside.

Liz and Ily said their good-byes, too, and wandered over to their section of the patio. The DJ had set up shop 100 feet behind them, making the view of the events picture-perfect.

Hatti was passed out cold, snoring, while a group of young girls walked by and made snide comments to one another. Liz flexed her muscles and whispered to a sleeping Hatti she would protect her body from evil, while she just lay there without a clue.

"Don't mess with her, I am a bounty hunter!" exclaimed Liz, having drank plenty of liquid courage that day.

"You keep an eye on her, Liz, while Kate and I use les toilettes," said Ily.

Liz flexed one more time showing her dedication to protecting Hatti's body, while she slept soundly, snoring poolside, and annoying most everyone around her.

Ily and Kate exited the restrooms and to the left, the smell of the grill, and sight of frozen drink concoctions, caught their eye. They had not eaten in quite a while, so they stopped to order a round of drinks appropriately named, It's Five O'clock Somewhere, and two quesadillas to share.

Liz woke Hatti up to eat when Ily and Kate returned to their chairs. They all needed something substantial in their stomachs, because a repeat of the day before was bound to happen the way they were drinking.

The DJ announced last call for folks to enter into the dance-off. He indicated a bar tab was up for grabs to the first place winner, a free bucket of Coors Light for second place. He then offered a swift kick in the ass for whoever was unfortunate enough to take third place.

Once the competition began, the DJ called up each participant one by one and had them introduce themselves to a captive audience. He called up a group of three men who performed acrobat stunts, flips, and kicks to the beat of the music. Up next was a young, slender brunette in a yellow bathing suit, and her short, overweight, blonde friend. They danced like the tramps they most likely were. Kate thought maybe they had taken the striptease dance class at Planet Hollywood.

Up next, the DJ gave a shout out for a tall, skinny guy wearing nothing but a banana hammock swim suit in electric blue, with a yellow lightning bolt across his ass. His resemblance to Steve Carell in, *"The Forty Year Old Virgin,"* was astounding. The crowd went wild when he emerged from behind one of the well-trimmed shrubs and strolled under the arch into his position in line.

"Last, but certainly not going to be least, Liz, from Wisconsin! Come on up here," called the DJ.

Liz put her hands over her mouth in sheer disbelief. Her eyes were wild. She sat frozen in the moment while her friends and the crowd around cheered. Some people stood on tip toes to see just what kind of competitor Liz would be.

Liz uncovered her mouth and looked at her friends.

"You are all a bunch of fuckers!" she shouted.

Not knowing how Liz would react, Ily and Kate had entered her into the competition while getting food and drinks. They waited for her to make a move.

Liz stood up and walked calmly to the front of the crowd and shook the DJ's hand. What happened next no one could believe. Liz pulled her swim suit up into her ass crack, galloped in front of everyone at the Paris pool and stood in line next to the 40 year-old, virgin. A roar of laughter and catcalls for each contestant were heard over the music, and the competition began.

The group of acrobats danced their hearts out. There was no doubt about their skill and talent. The routine was choreographed and performed with perfection. The crowd cheered pleasingly. They ended in a yoga type stance, joined together by arms and legs.

The pair of women took a few steps forward and the chubby blonde began to move. She thrust her hips, shook her ass, and made every inch of her move to the music. The brunette was a bit more reserved, twirling herself in circles, with arms held high above her head. They both grooved to the music for a few moments and the DJ called them back into line. A few men called out for more and the two girls smiled and licked their lips, tossing a piece of long hair over their shoulders.

The song changed to Madonna's hit, "Like a Virgin," and the man in the electric blue Speedo danced like nobody's business. He performed the running man, the lawn mower; he bent over, slapped his ass and ponied. He hit the cement patio and implemented a few break dance moves into his routine. The cheers, screams and hollers for this guy could be heard all the way to the Stratosphere. He danced his way over to the two girls that performed moments before and began humping the blonde's leg like a dog. This made every man and woman cry tears of laughter. He was a tough act for anyone to follow.

Liz had a look of determination in her eyes as the 40-year-old, virgin walked off the dance floor. She was up next. Liz tipped her head back, slammed her drink, adjusted her swim suit up her ass crack even further and did the moon walk to center stage. Her moves were raw. She shuffled around like a fish out of water.

Michael Jackson's, "Beat It," and Liz's performance had everyone from Le Café du Parc moving in their seats to the beat. Guests were enjoying their dinner and the show. Bystanders from the pool, hot tub, and patio clapped to the beat, whistled loudly and cheered, as Liz continued to win over the crowd. People up in the hotel windows peered down at the pool and witnessed Liz run to the 40-year-old, virgin, dry hump his leg, and then slap him across the face. She was having a hell of a time and making a complete ass of herself for the sake of winning the contest. When it was over, Liz ended with both hands raised high above her head and yelled out, "Wisconsin!"

The crowd at Paris pool cast their votes through cheers lured by the DJ. The 40-year-old, virgin took first place and Liz came in a close second. She definitely earned her free bucket of Coors Light. Kate, Hattie, and Ily hugged her and laughed. She was the winner in their minds.

People approached Liz throughout the day with high-fives, head shakes in disbelief of what they witnessed, and comments on her bold dance moves. She was a celebrity; at the pool anyway.

The four women continued to drink and mingle. The sun was sweltering and hydration was lacking for them all. Hatti mentioned that eating olives would help retain water and prevent dehydration, so she ordered a cup of olives and ate the majority of them herself. Beer and olives were not something the other women enjoyed. They obliged by sampling a few, but left the rest to Hatti.

The Paris pool closed at 7:00 p.m. and the four women stayed until the last minute, once again. They did not push their luck with the lifeguards this time, because they had a dinner date to prepare for. In honor of their last evening out in Vegas each woman had packed an extremely elegant gown. They wanted this night to be the most memorable.

CHAPTER 13

In the hotel room Ily took a bubble bath and shaved her legs, Liz washed her hair in the sink, and Kate lay on the bed waiting for her turn in the bathroom. Hatti wandered aimlessly around the room peering through slits in her eyes. She was swollen from the entire jar of olives she ate at the pool.

"How the hell am I going to see to put on my make-up? I can't even find my eyelashes!" she panicked.

Her friends laughed and teased her, indicating that at least she was well hydrated. She gave them the finger and lay down next to Kate on the bed with a cold washcloth over her eyes.

Sharply at 9:15 p.m., the four women strolled into Le Burger Brasserie. They stopped at the entrance to look around. All heads turned to gaze at the four women who just arrived. Nolan and his friends were seated at two pub tables to the right of the bar. The lights were dim, the music played at a moderate level in the background, and several televisions aired various sports games in progress. Nolan waved them over to where he and a group of men were seated.

"Wow! You look absolutely stunning," he said to Ily, giving her a kiss on the cheek.

Nolan turned to face Kate, Liz and Hatti, giving each of them a warm, welcoming hug. He introduced his friends and mentioned the drink special that evening was Dylan's famous daiquiri. They glanced toward the bar and a large, black man waved knowingly.

Within minutes, four of Dylan's famous daiquiris were placed in front of them. The men and women sipped cocktails and enjoyed deep fried chicken wings, onion rings and beer battered fries as an appetizer. The conversation was easy and the night was young. The men in suits were winding down from a long Saturday at the office and the four women were revving up for their last night in Vegas.

Nolan leaned over and gently placed a hand on Ily's thigh where her dress was slit revealing bronzed skin. She jumped at his touch, but did not move away. He looked deeply into her eyes again, just as he had at Toby Keith's bar. Then he spoke.

"You women look lovely this evening, Ily. I am guessing you do not intend to stick around the burger bar all night. What are your plans?" Nolan spoke, in a soft tone, and only to Ily.

She casually thanked him for the compliment and indicated they were going to make their way to Napoleon's martini lounge to listen to music, and then look for a place to eat dinner. She said they were all beat from a long couple days in the sun and a bit too much to drink.

Nolan and Ily turned their attention back to the group, but he never did move his hand from her thigh. Logic told her to move it for him and slap his face for treating her like another one of his bimbo, supermodel girlfriends. Her heart told her to let the rush take hold and see where it went.

Shane, Nolan's close friend, had been watching the interaction between him and Ily. He was curious to know who these women were when he could speak with Nolan privately. The first round of drinks went down smoothly. Hatti called out to Dylan to make another round of daiquiris, pronto.

"I have to use the restroom," Ily said, excusing herself from the group.

Nolan agreed to walk with her since it was across the casino. She assumed he had to use the restroom as well, but when she finished he was standing picturesque against the wall, focused intently on his Blackberry.

"Is it your wife or girlfriend that you are checking in with," asked Ily, catching Nolan off guard.

"Neither. I am still technically at work you know," he retorted.

Ily looked at him and laughed.

"Doesn't bother me what you are doing. Thank you for walking with me," she said.

As Ily turned to walk away, Nolan grabbed her arm and swung her around on one heel. He pulled her in close, a tear fell from his left eye, and he bent in toward her lips. She stood frozen for a minute and then reacted, squeezing him tighter and pulling him closer to her. She gently slipped her tongue into his mouth. He reciprocated and their tongues entwined, twirled and danced, back and forth, between his mouth and hers. They stood in the casino desperately needing one another. It felt so wrong, and yet, so right for both of them.

Nolan eased his grip on her, backed up a step, and gazed at her admiringly.

"You simply amaze me Ily. I have never met anyone like you," he said.

She was not sure what his words meant, but his kiss told her he wanted more of her. They walked, hand in hand, back to La Burger Brassiere. Ily released her hand from his just before they entered. Nolan did not know what to make of this, but rather than read into it, he followed closely behind. She led the way back to the group that was laughing and joking like old friends.

"What did we miss?" Ily asked, moving her eyes over her friend's faces.

Shane had told the other three women about a private party at Risqué night club and welcomed them to attend as his personal guests. He needed a code name to provide security upon their arrival. They had been discussing it and laughing at some of the ideas thrown out by the other men.

"Hollywood," said Liz. "Tell them our security word is Hollywood."

Nolan looked at Shane with caution in his eye. Shane told them there would most likely already be quite a few people entering under the code name, Hollywood, and to pick something else.

"Ok, how about Cee Cee?" said Liz.

Her friends looked confused by this choice, but nodded in agreement.

Shane laughed smugly and sent a message via his Blackberry to someone in charge of the private party.

"All set. Just let the people at the head table know you are registered under Cee Cee," Shane instructed.

Another half-hour passed by and Nolan excused himself for the evening. He had to get home to his daughters, but let everyone know the bar tab was available all evening, should they want to stay and socialize. Ily, Hatti, Kate and Liz also bid adieu, and made their way to Napoleon's martini lounge.

They found four open seats at the bar and asked about the drink special. The bartender handed out a wine list, but stated painkillers were on special. No one had ever heard of such a drink and decided to give it a try. It was Vegas after all.

A four piece band was playing light music and several couples were swaying to the beat on the dance floor. Napoleon's was a bit darker than the burger bar had been. Round, cherry wood tables and chairs with red velvet seat covers, hosted many guests that evening. There seemed to be a lot of men at Paris. This part the four women did not mind.

Four painkillers were placed on the bar. The dark red substance shimmered in the candle light and was unlike any drink they had ever experienced. It was a sensual drink the four women could not refuse. The warm contents in their glass slid down their throats like silk. It was going to be a short evening if they were not careful.

"Let's take a shot," insisted Ily.

"Are you kidding me," exclaimed Kate, "This drink alone is enough to knock me on my ass."

Ily laughed and summoned the bartender over to her. She ordered a round of shots and toasted to a splendid first, annual women's Vegas vacation. They clinked their glasses together, tipped their heads back and guzzled down what would be the first of many shots that evening.

Ily and Liz made their way to the dance floor together, while Hatti stayed at the bar flirting with the bartender. He had been seducing her since they walked in. Kate was mingling with the crowd and eventually took a seat with two women at a table across the room. Everyone was enjoying themselves immensely.

When the present song ended, Hatti made her way to the piano and dropped two, $20 bills into the glass jar with a request written on paper.

Hatti has been known to sing karaoke back home and her friends wondered what she requested. The piano player summoned her over to him, pulled the slip of paper from the jar and patted the bench next to him for her to sit down. She looked to her friends and obliged his request.

In the microphone he announced Hatti, from Wisconsin, would be bringing down the house with Carrie Underwood's hit song, "Before He Cheats". The men in the room went wild. Hatti and her friends assumed it was because of Carrie's beauty and sultry voice. Hatti hoped she could live up to their expectations. The music began and Hatti sang her heart out. The crowd sang along and when she finished Hatti was on her feet; so was her audience. She received a standing ovation. Liz, Kate and Ily chanted for the encore. The band struck up again, this time working Hatti's magical vocals to Michael Buble's version of, "Save the Last Dance." Hatti had a remarkable voice and delivered once again.

This was Ily's favorite song and at one point she was found on the dance floor performing the salsa. Her partner was a tall, dark and handsome, Latino man. His moves were on point and Ily followed his lead well. They were beautiful on the dance floor, their bodies entwined. Ily was having the time of her life. She lived to dance.

Once the song ended, Hatti took a bow and received a well-deserved applause from everyone at Napoleon's, including the band members. Ily made her way to the bar and chatted with Liz. Hatti found her way back to her friends, but Kate was missing. They scanned the room and found her seated at a table with two African American women, laughing, tipping over and hugging one another. Liz approached them and kindly excused Kate from the conversation.

"I don't want to go," Kate whined.

She was having a remarkable time with these two women and for once she was the center of attention. They listened to her stories, touched her arm lovingly and paid her many compliments. She would be damned if her friends made her leave such fun.

"How much did you have to drink, without us?" Ily asked Kate.

She stated she did not have any drinks, besides what they ordered together. All four women walked back up to the bar and finished the last of their painkillers. Kate said she was getting tired and dumped her supply of No Doze out onto the bar. She opened two packs and washed them down with her drink.

Smoothing her dress and fluffing her hair, Kate indicated that she was ready to go to dinner. Her friends could not believe Kate's behavior and were wondering what got into her. Maybe dinner would do her some good. She needed to sober up some or she would be hitting the sack soon.

CHAPTER 14

The steakhouse inside Paris was beautiful. The flowers were vibrant, the music was beautifully sung in French and the staff extremely hospitable. Nolan had informed the restaurant Ily and her friends would be arriving, so they prepared a special table just for them.

"I feel like a queen," Liz said, glowing from the inside out.

The waiter arrived at their table and placed the white linen napkins across each woman's lap. Then he poured four glasses of sparkling water and asked what the special occasion was. He was very cordial and had a slight accent. His hair was jet black and slicked, complimenting his big, dark eyes. He definitely fit the description of an Italian stallion.

The wine cart arrived table side, and each lady chose her favorite. Liz could not believe they were receiving such royal treatment. In the back of her mind, Ily wondered what all of this was going to cost. Kate was not cognizant of place or time and her eyes continued to open and close; so much for the No Doze working.

An hor dourve arrived next, along with four plates etched in blue and gold trim. The appetizer was appropriately named Portobello Stack. There were layers of roasted, sweet peppers, tomato cream, mushroom duxelles, artichoke, and boursin. The layers then repeated themselves. It was glorious to look at and was sure to be even more delectable to taste. Kate gazed at the succulent dish and quickly dug in her purse to take a picture of the exquisite display. She handed her camera to Hatti and asked her to take a picture of her with the hor dourve. Hatti complied and counted to three. Kate tipped the plate a bit too far. The Portobello Stack slid off the end and onto the floor.

"Fuck," she cringed, not knowing what else to say.

Hatti bent over in her chair and picked up what she could with her linen napkin. The mess was more than she could handle, but wanted to keep the mishap on the down low. A bus boy came to the rescue and cleaned up what Hatti did not.

Kate looked down at the ground and began to laugh. She was way too intoxicated to even care that she had just dumped their appetizer onto the floor. Then without notice, Kate slurred something and passed out face first in the mess that Hatti had just picked up.

"What did she say?" Ily asked the others, pulling Kate's face out of the slop.

Kate held her head up and used every ounce of energy she had to speak.

"I think I was roofied," she slurred, and slammed her head back down on the table.

Ily attempted to feed her water, but it just ran down the side of Kate's face. Hatti thought she should go back to the room and sleep it off, so Ily helped Kate pick her head up once again, stand from the table, and exit the restaurant. Ily gave her directions back to the room and handed her the key.

"Go straight to the room, Kate," Ily instructed.

Ily was reasonably sure she would make it on her own.

"You need to sleep this off girlfriend," Ily assured her, too intoxicated to know better herself.

Kate nodded and stumbled through the casino towards the elevators. Ily returned to the restaurant, not wanting to miss dinner.

"That was fast," Liz said. "Did you get her to the room?"

Ily said she gave Kate good directions and a room key, and then sent her on her way. Liz panicked and took off from the table in search of Kate. She needed to make sure she found the room and was safely put to bed. Hatti and Ily continued to drink wine and chat until the waiter arrived to take their order.

Hatti ordered the Angus Reserve Filet Mignon with roasted shallot and parmesan mashed potatoes, for Liz and herself. Ily ordered the Veal Filet Forestiere with wild mushrooms and garlic sautéed spinach. This was definitely going to be a meal to remember! They both hoped Liz would return in time to eat, while her food was hot.

"What about your friend who was sitting here?" asked the waiter.

Hatti and Ily laughed. They were thinking about the beautiful hor dourve sliding off the plate and onto the floor. They told the waiter she would not be returning, but Liz would be back shortly. He did not want to pry, so he thanked them, took the menus off the table, and returned to the kitchen.

Liz had returned from tucking Kate into bed and stated she thought that was the last they had seen of her for the evening. Moments later the waiter returned with their meals. The three women enjoyed every moment, savoring every bite. Their wine glasses were continuously filled and the waiter checked on them several times. He was intrigued by the women Nolan had sent to dinner that evening. It was a mystery as to who they were. After watching them throughout the evening he finally developed the courage to inquire.

"Which one of you is Nolan's wife?" asked the waiter.

Liz, Hatti, and Ily glanced at one another and laughed. They did not want to say too much, other than no one was his wife, but rather special guests for the evening. Little did they realize that in Las Vegas a special guest could be taken many ways.

When dinner ended the waiter thanked them, wished the women an enjoyable evening, and safe flight home in the morning. Ily was saddened by his words, because she did not want the weekend to end. Kate was missing their last hurrah and in the morning the fun would be over. Back to Wisconsin they would go.

CHAPTER 15

"Well ladies, we could go back to the room or head to Risque Night Club to check out the private party Shane told us about," said Hatti.

"I wouldn't mind seeing what a private party in Vegas is all about," replied Ily.

Kate nodded in agreement, so the three women headed toward the escalator that lead to the second floor of Paris. They were instructed to check in at the head table and would be shown the way from there. The ride up the escalator was exhilarating and nerve racking. The images in their mind of what lie ahead intimidated the women to no end. They had never been to a private party other than a wedding, funeral, or birthday back home. Everything about their stay in Vegas was a fantasy and attending a private party, under a code name, was just as fairy-tale-like.

When they reached the top of the escalator Ily, Hatti and Kate walked toward a table where three men in ties and sweater vests were seated. They assumed this is where they should check in and provide their code name.

Beautiful women in skin tight attire, stilettos and headdresses wandered around mingling with guests waiting to check in. The most illustrious woman in the bunch turned around and immediately recognized them.

From across the room she smiled, threw her arms in the air above her head and yelled, "Cee Cee? Oh my God girl is that you? Cee Cee, darling!"

She galloped over to the three women who were stunned by her open and heart felt welcome. They were not sure how she knew it was them, but thought it possible that Shane had something to do with it.

When the woman with the bright colored headdress met them face to face, for the first time, it became apparent that she was a man. He welcomed them to the Gay Pride convention and stated he was honored that Paris Casino was hosting the event. After all, everything is sexier in Paris.

Ily nudged Kate and said, "No wonder there are so many handsome men who smell like cake at this hotel."

"Call me Honey," he said, leaning in for a group hug.

The drag queen standing before them was gorgeous, but definitely packing the wrong parts. He explained the party was upstairs and his friend, Raven would be escorting them in. His head dress swayed side to side as he searched the parameter for Raven. Once he located her, Honey waved his way and Raven ran to meet the group. He greeted the three women with as much love as Honey had.

Honey put his arms around Raven's waist and said, "Raven, love, these are special guests of the beautiful men who run this hotel. Please be sure they arrive at the party and are shown to the bar."

Raven looked each of the three women standing before him up and down. He moved toward Liz, cupped her breasts in his hands, and squeezed.

"Oh my God girl, they look so real!" Raven squealed.

Honey agreed with a shake of his head dress and complimented Liz on her gorgeous breasts too.

"Enjoy the show darlings," Honey said, blowing kisses and prancing off to meet and greet another group who had just arrived.

Raven led the way past security and to the elevator. Hatti and Ily were discussing the scene around them and commenting on how beautiful the men in drag were. They were not sure how three, white women, from Wisconsin fit in the mix, but were willing to give just about anything a try.

A group of party-goers joined the three women, Raven, and security personnel in the elevator for the ride to the top. Hatti and Ily were snickering in the back and still in disbelief that the drag queens thought Liz was one of them. They mocked Raven over and over again, picking at each other's breasts and commenting on how real they looked.

Liz had enough of the whispering, turned around and yelled, "Shut up, you bitches!"

Raven exclaimed, "Oh, I just love how you talk to your bitches!"

Ily, Hatti, and the rest of the members on the elevator ceased their conversations and began laughing uncontrollably.

The elevator ride with transvestites was enough fun to last a life time. When the bell chimed signaling they had reached the top, the doors parted and in the dark room they could barely make out faces. The scent of the room was extremely alluring.

"Here we are, Cee Cee, darling. Enjoy yourselves and don't forget to look me up when the party is over. There is another gathering for VIP only," said Raven, in a deep, seductive voice.

Liz gave her a hug and led the way to the bar. After being felt up by a drag queen it was definitely time for a stiff drink. She ordered three double, lemon drop martinis to start.

With drinks in hand the three women circled the room. They were in awe of the gorgeous, gay men. They smelled so good, were well dressed, and talked about fashion, hair and the latest celebrities. What more could three women want!

Liz, Hatti, and Ily made their way to the back of the room, in front of a large stage. The crowd was facing that way in anticipation of a show to begin. The women gossiped about the men, were envious of those that made better looking women than they did, and wondered how on Earth they had found themselves there.

There was some shuffling behind the curtain that lined the backside of the stage. The crowd quieted and then a roar of excitement, cheers, whistles, and clapping consumed them. A woman in a gold sequin dress walked on stage.

If it were not a gay pride convention this man could have passed for a woman in any setting. He was beautiful. His legs were long, lean and stretched for miles beneath his sequins dress. His tanned skin was flawless. The gold coloring of his dress accentuated his tan and golden locks that hung to the middle of his back. It was the most beautiful mane any man or woman had ever seen.

"Wow, he makes Barbie look like shit," whispered Ily.

Hatti was whistling and cheering, while Liz and Ily stood motionless. The man in the gold dress was joined on stage by several other men, who looked like women. The show began with a few seductive interactions between actors and then the whips and chains came out. Hatti was having a hell of a time. She loved everything about sex and porn. This was pleasing her to no end.

Ily reached over and grabbed Liz's arm. She was drunk, uncomfortable, and wanted to flee the scene before them. Liz whispered to Hatti that she was taking Ily back downstairs and they could meet up at Napoleon's. Hatti was reluctant to leave after only an hour, but settled for the experience she had and walked to the elevator with her friends.

"I thought I was going to have a panic attack in there!" Ily told her friends on the way downstairs.

"It was a bit much for me too," replied Liz. "I could handle being felt up by the drag queen, walking the crowd and admiring the exquisite men, but when the dominatrix shit started on stage I knew it was time to hit the road."

The three women arrived at Napoleon's once again. They felt comfortable here and could relax, drink, and dance the remainder of the night away. They laughed and talked about their first experience in a room full of 900 gay men. What a sight that must have been. Three white women from Wisconsin, one who was mistaken for a drag queen, in a room full of gay men. Kate was sure to be disappointed in the morning, having missed all of this!

Hatti received a text message from the Harrah's bartender she had met on their first day in Sin City. He wished her a safe flight home and suggested she look him up on Facebook so they could get to know one another. Liz had met a man and was cozied up at a corner booth talking and flirting. Hatti hoped he was truly a man, which made Ily laugh.

"I am going to hit the sack," said Hatti. "I want to be rested for the flight home."

They walked over to Liz, told her they were off to bed, and asked if she was going to join them or her new friend. She looked at the man she was making out with; he had red lipstick all over his face. She thanked him and said good night.

The three women walked arm in arm through the casino. They were drunk, sated and blissful. Ily caught sight of the roulette table and wanted to have one last spin. She invited Liz and Hatti but they had enough of Las Vegas and were turning in for the evening. They kissed one another good night and Liz and Hatti headed for the elevators. Ily smiled, dug in her purse and pulled out $100.

"This is for you, Rita. One hundred dollars on red, sir," she instructed the croupier.

CHAPTER 16

The next morning the four women packed their belongings and took a cab to the airport. In line for security, Ily realized her driver's license and credit card were missing. She searched her suitcase, pockets, and purse.

"I don't know if they will allow her to fly back to Wisconsin without identification to get her boarding pass," said Hatti.

"If they know what is good for them they will grant her permission and bar her from ever coming back," laughed Kate. She unzipped the front pocket of Ily's carry-on revealing the missing documents.

The takeoff down the run way was smooth. The return flight on Allegiant was nowhere near as exciting as the flight out to Vegas. The Captain's voice over the loud speaker indicated cold temperatures and some snow in Wisconsin, but no delays in landing.

Liz and Kate paged through magazines, Hatti listened to music on her iPod, and Ily closed her eyes, sat back, and thought about the vacation from start to finish. She reflected on the flight to Las Vegas, the taxi ride to the hotel, their first night out at Toby Keith's Bar, a once in a lifetime mishap meeting Nolan and his friends, the horrible hangover, and bloody, busted up toe. The risky bet on Rita Red, handling counterfeit money, the move to Paris, and the dirty poolside seduction performance from Liz made her laugh aloud. She thought about the unique individuals they had met, stories shared, and laughing until they could not take anymore. The four women had been lifelong friends and now everyone they had met would be a part of their lives and memories, too.

Then Ily thought about her life back home and the dreadful existence she had been leading. She glanced over at Liz and realized she had been married twice and was now twice divorced. She was living her life to seek revenge on mankind. Hatti dated, slept with, and left many men, and had yet to find Mr. Wonderful. Kate was married and her roots were dug deep raising children and driving carpools.

Ily began to ask herself what truly kept her in the life she was living. Was it the thought of marriage ending in a 52% divorce rate? Or was it the thought of an atrocious sexually transmitted disease, while in pursuit of finding Mr. Wonderful?

Ily's phone vibrated on the drop down table in front of her. She flipped open the lid and saw one new text message. She wondered who would be texting her so early in the morning and thought maybe something had gone wrong at the office.

The text was from Nolan. It read, *"I enjoyed meeting you and your friends. I hope you made the most of your stay."*

Ily thought about his words for a brief moment. They all had such a wonderful time, but did they really make the most of their first, annual Vegas vacation together? She pondered this thought some more and decided the events that happened, the unusual, out of the norm encounters, and the stories they were taking home needed to be shared with family, friends and the world over. This trip was too good to keep inside her head.

Ily began searching through her purse for paper and pen, but found nothing. She turned to Kate and asked for something to take a few notes on.

Kate reached for the seat in front of her and pulled out the paper barf bag, handed it to Ily, and said, "Write away, Girlfriend!"

Would you like to see your manuscript become a book?

If you are interested in becoming a PublishAmerica author, please submit your manuscript for possible publication to us at:

acquisitions@publishamerica.com

You may also mail in your manuscript to:

**PublishAmerica
PO Box 151
Frederick, MD 21705**

www.publishamerica.com